RIDING FROM RICHMOND

THE PIONEER BRIDES OF RATTLESNAKE RIDGE, BOOK 4

NAN O'BERRY

Enjoy Pam
So glad you
could come
up
Nan

SWEET PROMISE PRESS
PO BOX 72
BRIGHTON, MI 48116

To the readers, I wish to thank you for taking the time to read this story. I hope you enjoy it as much as I do. Thank you.

PROLOGUE

Wanted

Nineteen-year-old refined lady from Virginia wishes to make the acquaintance of a genteel man of sweet disposition and means, with the ultimate goal of making a home in the western paradise of Rattlesnake Ridge. She is five foot and not afraid of hard work. Prefers a man of good moral faith but will accept any Christian Religion. Will correspond before deciding if the move is beneficial to both. If interested, please write in care of Miss McBride at P.O. Box 503 North Broad Street, Richmond Virginia.

CHAPTER 1

*I*t all began with this…..

THREE COWBOYS STOOD in front of the message board hung in the rear of Handley's General Store. Their earnest faces looking interested as they studied the bits of newspaper hung by nails below a large notice that read, *Messages for those wishing Matrimony.*

One tall, lanky cowpoke raised his right hand and pushed the battered Stetson away from his face. "Sure is a lot of 'em."

His remark brought an agreement of grunts from the two friends standing on either side of him.

"What 'cha make of it Dill?"

"Makes me wonder why they can't find fellers at home?" He remarked scratching his chin in the process.

"There's been a war, Dill. Fellers are in short supply. Now, Miz May said to come over here and look. There's got to be a likely candidate for the boss. I'm tired of spending eight days a week in the saddle."

"There ain't eight days in a week, Lou," Teddy spoke up. "Even I know that."

Lou's mouth pressed into a thin line. "Of all the times for you to develop brains," he grumbled.

"How come the boss can't find a girl around here?"

Lou's eyes narrowed. "You boys looked around lately? How many unavailable women you see pining for the boss to come courtin'?"

The other two men hung their heads.

"Yeah, I thought so. Besides, it can't be hard. It's just females." Lou's focus went back to the board. "Here look at this one." He pointed to the board.

Teddy narrowed his eyes and stepped close. "Lady wishes to marry. No children. No pets. Must be a fine upstanding member of society." He blinked. "I don't think this is a good choice. Seth likes his dog."

"Me either," Lou agreed.

"Here's one," Dill piped up.

"Shh, keep your voice down. We don't need Handley's wife poking her nose in our business."

Dill pointed to the newspaper clipping. "Husband needed. Respectable woman seeks male. Can cook and clean prefers a close proximity to town." He turned to look at Lou. "Is this proximity a disease?"

"Naw, means she wants to live near town. The boss lives around ten miles away."

"So, that'd be a no."

"That'd be a no." Lou nodded.

"Look at this," Teddy remarked. "Nineteen-year-old refined lady from Virginia wishes to make the acquaintance of a genteel man of sweet disposition and means, with the ultimate goal of making a home in the western paradise of Rattlesnake Ridge. She is five foot and not afraid of hard work. Prefers a man of good moral faith but will accept any Christian Religion. Will correspond before deciding if the move is beneficial to both. If interested, please write in care of Miss McBride at P.O. Box 503 North Broad Street, Richmond Virginia."

"She wants a lot," Dill pointed out.

"I think she just might do." Lou smiled. "She's

young enough. Wants to work hard. The boss will be plum happy to have her."

"What are you three up to?"

The tart voice made them jump.

Cautiously, Dill turned his head.

The round, face of Handley's wife confronted them.

"How do, Mrs. H-Handley," Dill managed to stammer out. "Nice day."

"Nice day," she mimicked. Her eyes narrowed as each of the boys turned. "What are you three up to?"

Lou pulled the newsprint from the board and slipped it into his pocket. "We thought we'd check out Winthrop's ads. Teddy here was thinking of getting a wife."

"Me?" The sheer terror in the young man's voice could not be hidden.

Lou sent an elbow into his ribs. "Oh, yeah." He gave a grin. "Yes, ma'am. Miz May sent us over here to check the responses, said it would do us good to find a nice wife." He lifted his hand and jerked it back toward the board.

The woman's eyes continued to glare as she lifted her hand and placed a fist on her hip. "And who would ever give you a second glance?"

Lou clapped his hands over the other cowboy's ears.

Teddy blinked.

"Aw, Mrs. Handley, a boy can dream. You wouldn't want to rain on young Teddy's desire to be a family man, now would you?" Lou smiled.

The woman crossed her arms and took a moment to think.

"I suppose not."

Lou took his hands down and Teddy put a finger to his ears to make sure he could still hear.

"Come on, let's get back to work."

"Yes, you do that."

The three made their way outside and to their mounts.

"Now what we gonna do?" Dill grumbled.

"Not to worry." Lou grinned. Lifting a hand, he patted his shirt pocket. "I got it all taken care of. Now, all we have to persuade Miss McBride to pack up and come west. If we're lucky, the boss will be besotted before we know it and ready to walk down that petal path. And us…" He slapped Dill on the shoulder. "We'll have two days a week all to ourselves."

"And how do you suppose we do that?" Dill asked.

"Well, we get us a smooth talker that knows what ladies like."

"Whose that gonna be?" Teddy piped up. "The only thing we talk to is cattle."

"Max. Max owes us one." Lou nodded. "Besides, Max has book learning. He'll know just what to say."

The three looked at each other with their smiles growing and mounted their horses to ride away.

CHAPTER 2

*S*everal Months later...
Spring 1874

MAX BARRINGER KNEW something was up the moment he arrived in Carson City. It didn't take a genius to realize that three top hands from the Circle N shouldn't be in town at the same time. He dumped the fifty pound bag of oats into the back of the buckboard; between the crates of block and tackle that he picked up for Cameron at the lumber mill. He then took a deep breath. His gaze followed the tall figure of Teddy Allen as he ushered his brother, Dill, and the ranch foreman, Lou Mason into the saloon down near the south end of town. Eyes narrowing, his curiosity rose.

"That's the last one," the storekeeper remarked.

Max turned his head and watched as the clerk from Carson City's General Store put a check on the pages held tight to his clipboard. Sticking it beneath his arm, the older man lifted his glance he gave a smile. "I think we completed the list in record time."

"Thanks, I know my boss will be pleased." With a nod, Max reached into the pocket of his trousers and brought forth a wad of bills. Stepping back to the clerk, he unfolded the money and counted out the bills.

"You'll need some change. Come on back inside."

Max followed pausing to step aside as two young girls walked past giggling as they made eye contact with him.

"Ma'am," he responded with a tip of his hat.

The giggling intensified as they disappeared onto the boardwalk that lined the main street of Carson City.

"Girls." The clerk shook his head. "I swear they are a disruption. If they didn't spend so much good money, I might ban them from the store."

Max pursed his lips but refused to comment.

Thank heavens his sister was still at the gangly age and preferred horseflesh to finding a beau. "Sure is busy."

The clerk glanced up as he pulled the change from the strong box. "Yes, a busy Friday. Stage is due in and its payday for some of the mines near here."

"Ah." Max gave a nod. "Yep, pay day was yesterday for those at Winthrop's back home."

"Oh, here from Rattlesnake Ridge are ya?"

"Yep, came in this morning."

"Here to see the sights and sounds of Carson City are you?"

"Something like that," Max grumbled.

"Your change, five dollars and thirty-nine cents." The clerk pressed the money into his hand.

Max shifted the change into his pocket and folded the bills in half before securing them in the same pocket.

"I guess that explains why the men from the Circle N are all in the saloon."

The hairs on the back of Max's neck bristled at hearing this.

The clerk gave a quick guilty glance across the street. "They been coming in once a month on a regular basis. Sometimes, they come in here get some chewing tobacco. Didn't come in this time. Been here two days, thought for sure they'd stop in once."

Max glanced over at the saloon. His brow knitted together as he lingered over the clerks unsettling words. "Ah, must have business elsewhere," he agreed. *Maybe,* he thought to himself, *a beer would taste good.* "I'll see you next time. Thanks for your help."

"Sure. Sure. Next time," the clerk murmured as he moved down the counter toward his next customer.

With a shake of his head, Max turned on his heel and hurried out the door. Drawn to the edge of the boardwalk, he stared across the street. It might be normal for Dill or Teddy to come in to town together, but not to have Lou with them. Rarely, did the three leave the Circle N without one of them at the helm, especially if Seth Nolan was out of town. All of it was just strange, especially if they had been there for two days. "Yep, mighty interesting."

He sauntered over to his buckboard and climbed aboard. Unwrapping the leathers from the wooden brake handle, he gave a flick of his wrist and woke the team from their slumber. "Let's head over and have a drink for the road." He then rode over to the bar and got down from the buckboard.

The doors parted as he strode into the saloon. The sign above the bar stated that a Big Bob Talbot owned the establishment. He glanced down the long mahogany bar to the man, who stood on the far end. He was a brute of a man judging from the upper half of him that towered over the bar. Max watched his gaze wander around the room with a hawkeyed stare as drovers, miners, and others drifted in.

Already, Max noted there were several poker games all ready in progress. "Poor souls will be broke again by tomorrow."

Finding a corner of the bar unoccupied, Max leaned against it and caught the bartender's eye. "Beer."

The big man gave a nod of his head as he flipped a clean mug over and filled it.

Max watched as it sent is sliding down the polished mahogany bar top toward him. He stuck out his hand and the mug came to a stop, the liquid sloshing from side to side."Thanks."

He placed two bits on the wood and turned around to check out the room. In the corner next to the window, he found them, huddled together, thick as thieves. Pushing away, Max walked over.

Dill heard the sound of his boots and glanced up.

"Howdy, boys," Max began. "This seat taken?"

The three men sat back. Their guarded looks betrayed them. Finally, Lou gave a shake of his head.

Max pulled out the chair. "Thanks," he remarked as he poured his body into it.

No one spoke as he took a sip of his beer. It gave him time to gather his thoughts. Then, he placed it on the table in front of him. The sound of the glass hitting the hearty pine wood had a ripple effect. One by one, each man lifted his chin to meet his glance only to shift their eyes back at the table top. Max leaned back against the chair and felt his brows arch. *Guilty everyone of them. But of what?*

"Alright," he drew out the word. "Who wants to tell me what's going on?

PERHAPS IT WASN'T the best idea to wear such a light color when traveling by stage. Caledonia McBride lifted the heavy white, cotton handkerchief her father had given her when he placed her on the train back in Richmond and brought it up to wipe the dust from her face. How she wished her father could have taken the journey with her.

"A lot of good this will do," she harrumphed as the stage rattled over the rutted ground releasing a new layer of fine ground up soil into the air. She brushed the bodice of her lavender colored traveling suit only to watch another cloud roll through the open windows. With a sigh, she let her hand flutter to her lap and made herself content to watch the country side roll by.

It had been a grueling two weeks of travel from her native Virginia to the Ohio River then from there she'd boarded a boat and sailed down to St. Joseph, Missouri. Next, it was a train ride to a small station in Dodge. The wheels against the steel tracks was loud, it nearly made it impossible to hold a quiet conversation with her fellow passenger. Still, it was better than the constant motion and dust from the wheels of the overland stage as it followed the old Pony Express route through the vast plains.

She hadn't realized the last part of the trip would take another three weeks. The first three days, she'd been shoulder to shoulder with other passengers. As they rolled north, the stage often stopped to pick up the occasional cowboy or miner. Caledonia found them wedged in any open space, at her feet, above with the luggage, and some had chosen to ride in the boot. Somehow, the real cowboys of the west had forgotten to tell the penny dreadful the true smell of the prairie. Her eyes closed as she recalled the odor of caked cow residue on their boots mingled with bodies that had gone days without submersion in water with a good helping of soap.

A spontaneous chuckle escaped her lips. "At least, the hard part is over."

She opened her eyes and leaned toward the window, holding the brim of her hat against the rush of the wind. Her gaze focused on the horizon. "In a few hours, I'll be in Carson City."

Her heart skipped a beat.

"And Mr. Seth Nolan will be waiting to take me to our home in Rattlesnake Ridge."

She pressed her palm against the wild throbbing organ in her chest and recalled the words from one of his letters.

How I long, dear, to show you the rugged countryside. Spring and summer find the prairies carpeted with wild flowers of every hue. I will pick you a bouquet worthy of a queen. You can stand and stare at the mountains draped in purple haze and thrill to the soar of an eagle as it finds its mate.

"Just as I have found you, dear Seth."

A smile played upon her lips, she closed her eyes and dreamed of hearing those words said, *I now pronounce you man and wife*.

"I CAN'T BELIEVE you were so stupid." Max groaned with a shake of his head. "What made you think you needed to play matchmaker for Seth?"

His sharp glare made all three cowboys hang their heads in shame.

"It worked for cows," Dill whispered.

"Yeah," Teddy chimed in. "You match them up by needs and wants."

"It seemed so simple," Lou echoed. "We used those lonely hearts, who been writing to Winthrop, and their letters posted in the General Store. We made a list and then marked out all the ones that were past their prime."

"Past their prime?" Max took a deep breath. "You fellows couldn't fight your way out of a wet corn sack. People are human beings not cattle. You can't throw two unsuspecting people together and expect them to marry."

"Winthrop don't have no trouble doing it," Dills said in their defense.

"You're not Winthrop," Max pointed out.

Lou shot him a murderous glare. "Ain't our fault old Seth, went off to buy a bull and ended up shackled, chained, and head over heels hitched to some pretty little filly in Cheyenne. If he'd just stuck to business, everything would be fine."

"Humph," Teddy groused. "If we'd known he was going to do this, we could have saved our money and a whole lot of trouble."

"Dear, Lord," Max groaned again. "What have you planned to do? Are you going to tell her?"

All three men glanced away from Max and stared into their beer.

"We were trying to come up with some more fancy words to say."

Max brows rose toward his hairline.

"You have no idea?"

Three heads shook.

"The only thing we can think to do is to save up to send her back."

"Yeah," Dill drawled. "But it took us six months to save to get her out here."

"I don't reckon she can live in the hotel for that long." Lou sighed.

Max rubbed his forehead with his left hand. If it wasn't so serious, he'd downright laugh, yet he couldn't. These were his friends and he owed them. "When is her stage due?"

"Coming in on the stage today."

Teddy's glum answer made each heart at the table sink.

"How much did it cost you to send for her?"

Dill glanced at Lou.

The cowboy sighed. "Near four hundred dollars."

"Four…." Max felt his jaw go slack.

"We saved nearly six months to get her the money so she could travel first class," Teddy explained. "We didn't want her to think old Seth was a slouch. She thinks she's marrying a real cattle rancher, one of them cattle barons."

"Lord a mercy…" Max sighed.

It was bad enough that they'd lied and wrote letters signing Seth's name, but to have a woman arriving thinking he was a cattle baron when the Circle N was just a middle sized ranch struggling to get ahead. Lord, they had sure exaggerated the truth. "You are in serious trouble," Max spoke low and leaned forward. "First of all, if Seth hears about this, he's going to have your miserable hides.

What you are going to have to do is explain to this woman exactly what's happened and send her back home."

Lou shook his head. "That's where the problem comes in. We don't have the money. I even sold my good saddle and all we raised is one hundred and forty-three dollars."

Dill nodded. "We can't even take her back to the ranch. Seth came back last night with his new bride and they are honeymooning. He sent us out to check the cattle and told us not to come back for at least a week."

"What are you going to do?"

"What can we do?" Teddy whined.

"Tell the truth," Max muttered as he watched the three cowboys look at one another in hopes someone had a better plan.

Lou shook his head. "Ain't fair to break a young lady's heart, Max, you know that."

"Should have thought about that before you sent for her."

"Look, Max, you are in this too." Lou's gravel voice was low. "Maybe you could lend us the money. We'll pay you back, honest."

Max shook his head. "I don't have that type of money and you know it. And if I did, I am not sure

I'd lend it to the likes of you three. You'd never learn a lesson."

Dill sent Max a murderous look.

Lou melted back against the chair. "Then, I guess one of us will have to go and break her heart."

Teddy eyes widened. "Not me, I don't know nothing about females. Let Dill do it. He's the ladies' man."

"You all should go," Max explained. "Don't let one mistake compound another. I hear tell confession is good for the soul." He lifted his glass and took a drink. "By the way, who wrote the letters?"

"We all did," Teddy explained. "Each of us wrote parts of them anyway. You helped."

"ME!"

Max's shout brought on a round of curious stares from those sitting nearby.

An uncomfortable silence followed.

Lou ran a hand around the lip of his glass. He glanced up, and then looked away. "Yeah, remember all those books you lent us."

Max felt his jaw go slack. "You didn't."

"All we did was use some of them phrases that Shakespeare fellow wrote."

Max felt his heart flip and drop to the toes of his boots. He shook his head.

"Hey, Max," Teddy began. "You could help."

Max eyed the three with caution.

Lou's eyes brightened. "You sure can. You got a sister and a ma."

Dill looked up expectantly in Max's direction, then added. "You know how those female minds work."

Max blinked. "Me? Don't pull me into this disaster."

"But you know our heart was in the right place," Lou pressed. "All we need is time, time to figure out a polite way of telling her how foolish we were."

"Time?" Max murmured, wondering where this was all going.

"Yeah…" Dill brightened. "You can help us with that right?"

"Oh, I don't know." Max looked around at the saloon.

"Think about the time your pa died. Why we gave up our free time and came over to your family and helped set up your spread. You had a mom tending to a younger child. What would have happened to you and your younger brother, Augustus, if we had said, *ain't our problem?*"

Max could feel the muscles on his face knot

together. "Not fair to use my own words against me," he grumbled.

"But we're right." Dill smiled, a glimmer of triumph sprinting across his expression. "We just need some help – like you did. You won't be getting your hands too dirty."

Max glared at them. "But they'll be dirty enough." He brought his hand to his chin and rubbed the skin there. "What would you have me do?"

Sensing victory, the three drew their chairs closer to the table.

"It will be easy," Lou began. "You just say that Seth can't be here."

"Yeah, take her out to the ranch you share with your family. You have good chaperones. Your ma won't let anything happen to her." Dill seconded.

"No one here in town or in Rattlesnake Ridge will see her," Teddy added. "That way, the gossips can't open their mouth. It will be on the up and up."

Lou nodded. "While you're doing that, me and the boys will raise some more money by rounding up some horses and selling them to the army. Then we can come by and break the news about Seth marrying his long time love and give her the money and send her home."

"Long time love?"

Teddy waved his hand. "We'll be the only ones to know it was love at first sight on Seth's part."

"It' a great plan. You're a fine friend to help, Max," Dill spoke up.

"Now wait one minute…" Max pushed away from the table. "You boys need to come clean."

"We will. We sure will. You helping us out for a bit will be just great." Lou nodded.

"Besides, she's gonna be awful tired after that long ride," Teddy piped up.

"Yeah…" Max fumed.

"She'll need some place to rest. Even if we was to tell her."

"Rest," Max echoed.

"Then you'll do it!" Lou grinned. "I knew we could count on you!"

Max opened his mouth but nothing came out. At that precise moment shouts came from the street and the sound of wagon wheels grinding to a halt echoed the coming of the stage. The conversation ceased.

"That's the stage," Dill whispered.

All heads turned toward the saloon doors.

"You're a pal, Max." Teddy grinned and bound to his feet, pushing his chair back.

"We won't forget this, will we fellers?" Dill's grin split his face from ear to ear as he joined his brother.

"Owe you one," Lou murmured and stood extending his hand.

Max stared at the open palm. A cowboy shake was as binding as signing your name to a contract. But no matter how he looked at this, there was no way out. He stared at Lou's hand, then with a surrendered grin extended his own.

Lou's grasp was strong and binding.

Max stared at his palm when the cowboy let go and wondered why he didn't see a brand for losing his mind left on his palm.

One by one, the men filed past him each giving him a good thump on the back.

"I don't even know her name?" Max called out.

"Oh, that's easy."

Max turned in his chair and stared at the three cowboys standing at the door.

"It's Caledonia McBride," Lou answered.

In a blink of an eye, they were gone leaving him to try and wrap his mind around what he'd gotten himself into.

"I must be plumb loco."

CHAPTER 3

I ought to have my head examined. Max reminded himself for the second time as he pulled his rig to a stop at the stage depot. *Ought to tell her the truth, darn the consequences and hang those three make-believe matchmakers out to dry.*

But he knew he wouldn't. Lou, Dill, and Teddy had helped him save his ranch when his father died on a roundup. The men his dad hired quit as soon as his body was in the grave, leaving two hundred head of cattle milling around with no place to go. They, along with Seth, stepped in to help when everyone else turned their heads.

He owed them.

Glancing at the people milling about, he sighed

and wrapped the leather reins about the handle of the brake and climbed down.

"I won't be long," he muttered to the team. Staring at the building, he murmured. "Caledonia McBride – what kind of name is that?" With a sigh, he shoved his clenched fist into the pocket of his trousers and with his shoulders hunched, he walked into the bright yellow building.

It took a few moments for his eyes to adjust from the bright sunlight outside. He could see farmers picking up crates of chickens. A few towns' people meeting family and friends. There was even a rousing checker game going on in the corner of the room behind the potbellied stove that would sit idle until winter. A figure caught his eye.

Small in stature, clad in a soft lavender outfit, and bathed in a shaft of sunlight, she looked more like an angel than a mail-order bride.

He struggled to swallow the lump in his throat. When his resolve grew, he plowed through the middle of the humanity. "Excuse me," he began, as he came to a stop before her. "Ma'am? Ma'am, are you Miss McBride?"

The large brim of the satin bonnet began its slow rotation upward. Beneath the edge or the gathered ribbon, a heart shaped face that seemed more blue eyes than anything else peered up at him.

Max could have sworn someone gave him a sucker punch right to his middle. His lungs seemed to stop functioning. He tried to remember how to breathe. All he could do was to gaze down, mystified at how deep those endless pools of blue seemed.

Oh, how they resembled the color of the Nevada skies above. His mouth opened but nothing emerged. He watched her face brighten.

"Mr. Nolan?" There was no denying the excitement in her voice as she held out her hand.

Max blinked and then grew sober. Remembering his manners, he reached up with his right hand and whisked his hat from his head, holding it by the brim with both hands to keep from grasping what she held out to him. "N-no." He cleared his throat and spoke in a stronger voice. "No ma'am." This time the tone was more convincing.

"Oh." Her face seemed crestfallen and her hand fell to her lap.

His stomach plummeted to his boots. Without thinking, Max reached out, pausing halfway only to pull his hand back to his hat brim. "I'm afraid I have some bad news."

Her face grew ashen. "Has something happened to him?"

Max swallowed. He could tell her the truth. Instead, something else came from his lips. "No ma'am, he –um- he's not in town."

Her eyes widened. "Not in town. He knew I was coming."

"Oh, yes ma'am." He nodded. "He had some pressing business he had to take care of."

"Oh."

Well, it wasn't really a lie. Having a brand new wife was indeed pressing business. In the recesses of his mind, Max heard his subconscious laughing. Shrugging it off, he smiled. "I came to get you."

Her gaze riveted on his and to Max's surprise, his heart took an extra beat. "You'll be staying at my ranch, till he can get back."

"Oh, I …." She glanced at the floor. "I was afraid he'd gotten cold feet."

"No ma'am, he hasn't forgotten." There was no disguising that lie. Max waited for the lightning bolt to strike. Lucky for him, nothing happened.

Her smile broadened. "Good, I'm glad for that. I'm looking forward to meeting him."

Max wanted to look anywhere but at her face.

"I'm sure." He took a moment to gaze around the room. "Are you ready to go?"

She nodded.

"Is this your bag?" Max motioned at the small carpet bag lying at her feet.

"Yes. Along with this trunk."

He glanced at the small wooden box she was sitting on. It wasn't big. In fact, it seemed awful small to hold the contents of a person's whole life. "I'll come back and get that once you're in the wagon."

"Very well." She grasped the handle of the bag and handed it to him.

Their hands touched.

A delightful warmth spiraled up his arms shocking his system.

She must have felt it too, for her cheeks grew pink, as pink as his mother's peonies that grew in the box beside the front porch. "Thank you," she whispered.

He gave a nod and shifted the bag in the other hand before he took a light grip upon her elbow. "Shall we?"

Propelling her forward, they moved through the dwindling crowd neither speaking until they reached the wagon. Max stepped forward and swung the carpet bag into the well in front of the seat. She reached up to grasp the metal handrail in an effort to haul herself to the wagon. Her petite height made the grab a bit more difficult.

"If you'll pardon me," Max mumbled. Before she could reply, he stepped close, slid his arm beneath her shoulders and drew her body against his. His other hand slid beneath her knees and in a flash, she was in his arms. The movement drew her off balance and she flung her arms around his neck. He heard her inhale sharply at the contact.

Lord, she smelled of lavender or was it lilac? It didn't matter. Max took a good long sniff.

"The seat?" she whispered.

"Oh, yeah." As gently as he would have lifted a baby bird to its nest, Max swung her into the wagon.

"Th-thank you," she stammered.

Max stepped back and rubbed his hands down the sides of his trousers as if trying to get rid of her feel. "I-I'll be right back with your trunk."

Turning on his heel, Max fled. One thought only echoed in his head. *I have truly lost my mind.*

CALEDONIA SAT stunned and waited for her heart to calm its thunderous beat. She hadn't expected him to him to gather her in his arms. Startled at first, she'd thrown her arms about his shoulders. The way she was cradled in his arms put her gaze level with his own. She gulped recalling the warmth in his brown eyes. They reminded her of the color of caramel she'd gotten one Christmas and wondered if his lips would carry the same salty sweet taste. Just the thought caused a rise of heat that seemed to flood her cheeks. Oh, how she wished she'd placed her fan in her reticule instead of packing it in the trunk. Straightening her shoulders, she adjusted the bow that held her hat against her head.

I'll claim it is just the afternoon heat, she told herself. A bubble of laughter echoed in her brain but it proved short-lived as her new-found friend exited the depot with the trunk. "Careful," she murmured as he and the stage hand lifted it onto the back of the wagon.

With a grunt, he shoved a stack of burlap wrapped seed forward and slid the trunk to a secure spot on the corner of the flatbed. "Thanks," he said to the clerk. He brushed his palms down the front of his shirt.

The clerk looked at Caledonia and smiled then

touched his hat before disappearing back inside the building.

She watched him as he moved around the back of the wagon to the front wheel on the other side. His hands reached for the rail and in a fluid motion, he swung into the seat beside her.

Nervously, she looked forward not wanting him to see her interest. To keep from staring, she arranged her skirts tighter around her so that he would have plenty of room.

"Here we go," he announced.

Her heart was picking up its beat as he brought the leather reins down on the horse's rump. A slight jolt followed as the animals leaned against their harnesses and pulled the heavily laden wagon forward. Merging with the mounted riders and buggies, they headed out of Carson City and toward the towering tree covered mountains in the distance.

Minutes turned to hours as they rode further away from town. With each passing mile, Caledonia began to relax. The long grasses bent their heads toward the ground as the breeze passed over them. A soft sweet scent wafted up and she took a deep breath inhaling it for a lasting memory.

"Enjoying the ride?"

His voice startled her. Pressing a hand to her

hat, she turned to find him staring at her a soft smile touching his lips turning the edges upwards.

"I am."

He gave a flick of the reins. "It's pretty country. Especially in spring. We've had a good wet winter so the grasses and flowers have bloomed."

"It is that," she agreed.

"I don't think I mentioned my name. I'm Maxwell Barringer. My friends call me Max."

"Hello, Max. I'm Caledonia McBride." She stilled and blinked. "I guess you know that."

"Yes, ma'am, they told me your name."

"They?"

He suddenly glanced away. "Mr. Nolan. He and his drovers, when they came over and asked for my help, before going out to the herd."

His voice seemed nervous and his explanation a bit rushed. She overlooked it as being nervous. "Well, my friends call me, Callie."

"I like that. Callie," he repeated her name.

Caledonia felt a burst of pride. She didn't want the conversation to die. Quickly, she thought of another question. "Have you lived here all your life?"

Max gave a nod. "My parents came as homesteaders. My father worked for the lumber operation in Rattlesnake Ridge till he had the down payment for some land southeast of the lake. We live closer to the trail that leads into town. I do some odd jobs for the lumber mill, like my dad. The mill's run by Winthrop. He sponsored the ads for the mail-order brides."

He gave her a nervous glance. "That's why I was in Carson City, some supplies they don't have in our smaller General Store. Had to get them brought in you know."

"I see." Her lips twitched a bit bemused.

HEAVEN HELP HIM, he was running off at the mouth like a school kid. Max stole a glance in her direction. "I guess you've seen bigger back where you come from."

Now, it was Caledonia's turn to smile and nod. "I have, but that was a long time ago." Her voice grew melancholy. "Back before the war, my hometown was big and prosperous."

"What city was that?"

"Richmond. Richmond, Virginia," she replied and gazed off at the horizon. "But the war ended all that. Now, it's mostly in ruins or in the rebuilding stages."

"I heard it was rough back there."

"Yes, it is. There's no future left for many families. Money is a precious commodity in the south with few businesses, there is no way to make a living. Plantations have been broken up for smaller farms but the rent was so high, few can afford it. Everything takes money. So, it takes time. But in all honesty, it will never be the same."

Max grew quiet listening to her words. He could almost feel the desperation in her voice. "I'm sorry."

She shook her head. "Don't be. It was a very stupid war." She brightened. "That's why I was so excited to accept Mr. Nolan's offer and come out here, to begin my life over in this beautiful part of the country."

Max grinned back at her, "I think it's the best part of the country. You'll love it in the summer time. Winter is pretty too, all the snow. Do you get much of that in Virginia?"

"No, not too much. Our summers can be long and so very humid. I'm looking forward to the change."

They rode along in the quiet, their bodies swaying with the movement of the wagon.

"What did your family do back there, in Virginia?" Max questioned.

"My father is a farmer. We once had over three hundred acres most of it in corn and tobacco."

"What happened to the farm?"

"Lost it to taxes. There weren't any buyers for the crops we could harvest. My father gave up and moved to the city, hoping to find work."

"Did he?"

She shrugged. "Some. He was hired by a warehouse down in Shockoe Bottom. We lived in a room above the business."

The conversation lagged for a bit.

"I see," he murmured. "So you gave it all up to come out here to become someone's wife."

"I did."

They listened to the plodding steps of the team before Max spoke again, "Don't they have young fellas in Virginia?"

Caledonia's smile faded somewhat. "A few, but they are either too old, dead, or still way too young for matrimony."

They both chuckled.

"The war took most of the young men. Those that returned are finding it hard. Taxes have taken the land and there is little money to purchase the old farms. Even if they do buy the land, the work is hard and with the prices, there seems to be no incentive to stay on the farm. Many that are sound have headed west or gone to the goldfields in California in hopes of a better future."

"I understand about prices and the lure of the big city. Still, that sounds more exciting than ending up here in Rattlesnake Ridge."

Caledonia took a deep breath and stared at the meadows, the trees, and the endless blue sky. "I guess it could be, but it doesn't excite me. I want to be in a new place to set down roots and watch the community grow."

"Well, you can watch things grow out here," Max mused. "But they are mostly trees and cattle."

"Trees and cattle are good." She smiled.

They lapsed into silence and the sun warmed her back. In an effort to catch the breeze, she lifted her hand and removed the ribbon that held her bonnet in place. The breeze shifted over her and she turned her face to greet the sun.

"Might want to put that bonnet back on. Your skin is so fair; you might get a little burnt."

Caledonia relaxed and took a deep breath. "In a minute, I just want to breathe the freshness of this air." She turned to face him. "Back home in Richmond when everyone fires up their stoves, a thick gray pall hangs over the town and everything, your clothes, your hair, your food smells of wood."

Max's eyes widened as he digested her words. "Hadn't thought about that."

Leaning back against the seat, she placed her hands in her lap. "I think I'm very glad I came," she whispered. "I hope Seth will be pleased with me. Do you think he will?"

Just the way she asked the question brought a wave of jealousy swiftly to Max's heart. For some reason, he didn't want Seth to know about her. He didn't want Seth to fancy himself as a ladies' man with two women fighting for the chance to marry him. His jaw flinched. "He'd be a fool not to."

Suddenly, Caledonia's hand was upon his arm. The warmth of her palm burned straight through the cotton of his shirt scalding his skin. "I'm so glad you think so."

Max swallowed the lump that formed in his throat and he felt like the biggest turncoat in history. "Yes, I think so."

With a flip of the reins he coaxed the horses to move faster. The faster they trotted, the quicker he could get home. The quicker he could get home, the sooner Lou and his buddies would come through with their cash and pretty little Caledonia McBride would be out of his life for good. The thought had both joy and pain, but it would have to do.

They horses moved through an overhead arch with the word Barringer burnt into the wood, on either side a diamond with a B in the middle signaled their brand.

"This marks the beginning of our ranch."

Caledonia shifted in the seat and craned her head back to catch a better glimpse of the sign. "Diamond B," she murmured.

"Our brand," Max explained. "Each of our horses and cattle are marked to tell the difference between the herds. Our fence doesn't go around the two hundred acres we own, but we have markers set up every mile, so folks will know. Cattle." He shrugged his shoulders. "Well, they don't read so well. They'll wander around a bit and mingle with the other ranches near about, so we brand them in the spring and keep a tally of the herd."

"Other ranches do the same?"

He gave a nod. "Common practice." He gave a motion forward with jerk of his head. "The closer you get to the ranch, the more likely you are to see a fence line. We have pastures for each season, winter we bring the herd closer to home."

"You keep saying we, do you have a lot of help?"

"I have a big family, my brother, Augustus, and my sister, Melinda help out when I'm up on the mountain. We employ five hands that work during the spring, summer, and fall with my brother. He's in charge of the ranch while I'm working at the mill."

"So you do two jobs?"

"Sometimes, the lumber operation gives me a steady income and helps keep the ranch running. One day, I'll quit and work with Augustus. But right now, every penny we can save means upkeep on the house, the land, and the cattle. Besides," He sighed. "I like being on the mountain."

"I see, and do the hands that work with your brother stay year round?"

He shook his head. "Come winter, one or two leave for work on other ranches south of here."

"I find it interesting that your sister helps out."

"Yeah." Max gave a slight grin. "Melinda is as a good a rider as anyone else. She can work cattle and is great with horses. You'll find women have a lot more duties out here than back in Richmond."

"I do say," Caledonia exclaimed. "This will be an eye-opening experience."

"Whoa."Max pulled back on the reins and

pressed the brake causing the wagon to still. "There it is," He pointed across the meadow to the gentle rise and the two-story log cabin perched on the knoll.

Caledonia's breath caught. "Oh, Max, it's beautiful."

He couldn't help the smile that streaked across his face. "Yeah, it is." With a whistle, he released the brake and eased the taut leather and the horses moved smartly toward home. The closer they moved to the log cabin nestled against the tall fir trees, the more his mind twisted on how he planned to tell his mother about their guest. Before he could figure a good explanation, a wild war whoop echoed across the grasses. He turned this head to see a buff colored buckskin racing toward them, the rider leaning close to the horse's neck, a long blonde pony tail snaking out behind her like the tail of a kite.

"Here comes Melinda now," he spoke.

"Max!" She cried and pulled her horse to a sliding stop. Her gaze moved from him to the woman sitting beside him on the wagon. "Howdy." Her glance flickered to her brother. "Didn't know you were bringing a guest home."

"Didn't quite know myself." Max felt the heat

rise in his cheeks. "Melinda, this is Miss Caledonia McBride."

"Hello, Melinda, please to meet you." Caledonia smiled broadly.

"Please to meet you too." Melinda gave a nod. "How'd you meet my brother?"

Caledonia turned and smiled at him. "Your brother was kind enough to invite me to the ranch until my future husband can come and pick me up."

Max eyes grew wide. He caught his sister's confused glance and looked at his feet.

"Future husband," she mumbled.

"Yes, Seth Nolan."

Melinda's eyes grew wide as she let out a little gasp. "Seth? Why he —"

"Got to go, Mel, I have to get these supplies to Ma. See you later." Max snapped the leathers and with a toss of their heads, the horses leaned hard against their yokes and broke into a trot.

He left his sister with her mouth hanging open. He couldn't risk waiting for her to follow. Max didn't dare want her to begin poking into his business. Nope, the sooner he got Caledonia to the house, the sooner she could settle in and he could figure a way out of this mess.

CHAPTER 4

*B*ethany Barringer heard the wagon roaring into the yard. Dropping the towel over the bowl of rising dough, she proceeded to dust her hands on her apron and marched toward the back door. "Augustus," she called out. "If you are running those horses through my chickens." She flung the door open. "You and I are going to have a long..."

Bethany stepped onto the porch and drew up short. To her surprise, Max thundered in pulling the team to a stop with a cloud of dust hot on his heels. She glimpsed a young woman beside him, one hand grasping the metal bar around the seat, the other holding tight to the hat that threatened to take flight. The horses clamored to a halt and gave a toss of their heads in complaint as they came to a stop.

"Maxwell?" She could feel her brow knit together as she moved from the porch to the yard.

Her son gave a sheepish glance in her direction.

Any question that she'd been prepared to ask was quickly bitten back.

"I've got your supplies, Mother, along with those Mr. Cameron needs at the timberline."

She plastered a smile on her face. "Thank you." Her gaze strayed to the young lady sitting beside him still gathering her wits. "Max?"

He swallowed heavily and adverted his glance.

Her eyes narrowed.

A tinge of pink appeared in his cheeks. "Mother, I'd like for you to meet Caledonia McBride. She's going to spend a few days with us on the ranch."

"A few—"

Her oldest boy swung down from the wagon. The set of his lips told her he was none too happy to be in this situation. She waited as he moved around to the young lady's side and helped her to dismount. His hand upon her elbow, he led Caledonia toward his mother.

"Mrs. Barringer," she murmured and held out

her hand. "I'm so sorry for the imposition. It really is just a few days until my intended comes for me."

Her brows arched. "Your intended?"

"She's come a long way, Mother. I'm sure she'd like to rest before dinner."

"Yes," Bethany replied in a shocked tone. She gave her son a blistering glance then stepped forward to take Caledonia's hand. "Around here, folks call me Bethany. Welcome to the Diamond B, Caledonia."

"Please, call me Callie." Her smile broadened as she relaxed. "I hope it's no trouble."

"None." Bethany stole her arm around the young girl's shoulder. "I never know what Max is bringing home. Last year, it was a pair of matched horses." She glanced over her shoulder and gave her son a stinging glare, before she ushered her guest toward the front door. "You're much prettier and easier to please than those two brutes were. So, where did you say you were from?"

"Richmond," Caledonia replied.

"As in, Virginia?"

The girl at her side nodded.

"You've had a long journey. Come, I know just the trick, a cup of tea and a nice nap. Max, you bring her things into the house and put them in the room beside your sister."

"Yes ma'am."

Max stood in the ranch yard and waited until the front door closed before he gave a sigh of relief. Turning back to the wagon, he knew he would pay for this momentary lapse in good judgment. He hurried around to the rear and put the tailgate down. The supplies would wait. Right now, he needed to get Caledonia's things moved into the room before Mel or Augustus decided to meddle into his business. He glanced at the empty barn door.

"Not a ranch hand in sight."

His mouth twisted and he reached for the trunk dragging it against the wood. The sound was like the wail of a banshee. It flowed up his backbone causing his skin to pimple. Despite his best attempt to hide it, he couldn't help but shiver.

"Hey, boss, could you use some help?"

His head jerked up and he spied one of his errant crew.

Red leaned against the open doorway, his dome

hat pushed back allowing a shock of red hair to flow across his forehead. His thumbs hooked in the loops of his trouser. His face nearly split in two by the broad toothy grin.

Max's mood soured. "Never did like being the butt of anyone's jokes," he muttered. Another glance to the cowboy and he asked, "You going to stand there all day, or you plan on earning your keep?"

Red looked around as if searching for his comrades. Unhooking his thumbs from the wide belt at his waist, his long arms dangled at his sides as he pushed away from the barn opening. "Nope. Hadn't planned on it. All you had to say was you needed some help."

Grumbling beneath his breath, Max waited while the cowboy sauntered over to the rear of the wagon. "Grab the other side, will you, Red."

The cowboy reached for the opposite end of the trunk and they lifted it from the wagon bed. "You know, Boss, we kind of thought you were going for supplies." Red grunted as the weight of the trunk and its contents swung free. "Had we known you were bringing home the two legged kind, we might have gone with you to give you our list."

Max shifted to a quick stop. A turn of his head

and he leveled a narrow glare at the cowboy across the wooden trunk.

Red had the decency to try and give an honest expression before looking at the ground. Still, there was no mistaking the laughter in his eyes.

"Let's get this inside shall we?"

His tense tone faded the mirth in Red's face. "Yes, sir, boss. Anything you say."

Grumbling, he led the way across the yard and up the porch to the main house. His luck held for his mother had only pushed the door against the jam. Max paused to shove his hip against thick heart of pine and it fell back, banging against the table against the wall making the china bowl rattle.

"Maxwell Barringer, don't you dare bust a single wall!"

He could feel the heat pool in his ears as Red snickered. "Yes, ma'am." He shot Red a furious glare and the cowboy looked away. "Watch yourself."

"Yep," Red grunted, but kept his eyes adverted.

With great care, the two men wove their way through the living room and up the stairway to the four bedrooms upstairs. They paused at the landing to shift the trunk in their grasps before moving forward.

"Women sure do carry lots of things," Red remarked.

Max could only nod. "Room in the middle," he said with a nod of his head toward the door on their left.

Once the door was opened, they turned parallel to the opening and Max backed into the room.

"Where do you want to put it?"

"Foot of the bed," Max grunted.

As gently as possible, the two set the trunk in place then backed away.

"How long she gonna stay?" Red asked.

Max shrugged his shoulders. "Not sure. At least a couple of weeks."

Leading the way, Max moved from the room. "That's sure gonna put a hitch in your giddy-up."

Ignoring the comment, Max moved down the hallway. "Let's get the supplies into the kitchen."

The two made their way back down the stairs.

At the foot, he could see his mother pouring tea. "I'll be right with you." Dusting his hands against the side of his trousers, Max moved toward the large table in the dining room off the main living area. The huge oak table his father had handmade could easily sit six comfortably. He paused at the end and grasped the back of the chair. How small

Caledonia appeared. He waited while his mother took her seat.

"Thank you for your hospitality," Callie spoke softly.

Her words were soft and soothing against his ears.

"You are very welcome, my dear," his mother murmured. "Sugar?"

She picked up the bowl filled with the cubes and held it out to her guest.

Callie scooped two out and placed them in her cup. Under his gaze, she picked up the silver spoon and stirred the contents. Her arms were so small; he wondered how she had the strength to churn butter. Watching her so intently, he didn't see his mother gaze in his direction.

"Oh, are you joining us, Max?"

Her question jolted him back to reality. He shook his head. "No, ma'am. I just came over to let you know the trunk is at the foot of the bed." He used his head to jerk toward the open doorway. "We're going to bring in the other supplies to the kitchen."

"Oh, good."

He caught Callie's shy gaze and their eyes locked. Max didn't want to turn away.

"Thank you again, Max."

His mother's voice broke into his stupor. His gaze never strayed, but his mouth lifted to an easy grin. His next words were spoken for his mother's benefit, but he hoped Callie would take them to heart as well, "No problem. Enjoy your tea. I will see you at supper, Mother."

She nodded.

Callie blushed as she picked up her cup in both hands and lifted it to her lips.

He watched mesmerized.

"Max."

He blinked.

"The supplies," his mother prompted.

"Oh…" He grinned. "Yes."

One last long look and he hurried from the room.

BETHANY WATCHED her son move through the door. An audible sigh from the young lady seated across from her reached her ears. Turning, she began, "So, you came out to be married."

Caledonia glanced over to her. A slight blush reached her cheeks.

"Yes, that is the plan."

Bethany nodded.

"If I may ask, how did you meet?"

"Through letters. I saw his ad in the newspaper and we began to write. His words were so wonderful. The descriptions of the hills, the land, even some of the people he'd meet. I felt as if I'd known him all my life. Then, when he asked for my hand in marriage, it seemed so natural."

Callie shifted her gaze to the cup. Under Bethany's scrutiny, she turned the cup around and moved her thumbs over the Blue Willow design. She waited and finally, the young woman looked up.

"You-you must think me a bit foolish." Her voice lowered. "I mean to come all the way out here, not knowing the man who I am to marry except for his letters."

A motherly smile crept into Bethany's features. "Oh, I wouldn't say you were foolish. I'd think your actions are very brave."

Her cheeks turned the color of a bright red apple. "It feels a bit silly now," she admitted. "I mean he wasn't even able to meet me. I hope he hasn't gotten cold feet." She glanced over the table her eyes filled with concern. "He is out of town on business...or so they said."

"Who said?"

She swallowed. "Well, Max."

"Max." Bethany's brows rose in surprise. She sat back and took in the information before speaking once again, "Did he know you were coming?"

Callie lifted her shoulder in a slight shrug. "The train from St. Joseph got held up due to part of the track being washed away in a storm. We spent a week waiting. I can only assume that he thought I wasn't coming. So he went away on business. I hope he won't be too mad when he finds that I have arrived."

"Well, it can be explained once you two get together." Bethany leaned forward and patted her hand. "Let's not make mountains out of mole hills."

Callie seemed to relax. She blinked then raised her hand to cover a deep yawn.

"There, there," Bethany crooned. "Here I am asking questions and you are dead on your feet. Let me show you to your room." She stood as did Callie.

"I apologize. I'm just so tired."

"Of course you are. A train through the prairie then a stage coach ride. You have a right to be tired." Bethany rounded the table and placed an arm around her young protégé. "Once you get upstairs, you can lie down and nap. I'll wake you in time for the evening meal."

"Are you sure? I should be helping you."

Bethany held up her hand, silencing her. "I won't hear of it. You follow me." She led the young woman up the stairs and to the bedroom next to hers. Pushing open the door, she smiled. "Here are your things. Make yourself at home."

She watched as Caledonia moved past her and brushed her fingers across the quilt that covered the double bed.

"What a beautiful quilt."

"Do you sew?"

Caledonia nodded. "I do, but I haven't made a quilt in years."

"Well, we'll have to remedy that."

Caledonia looked back and smiled. "I'd like that Mrs. Barringer."

"It's Bethany, dear." She turned back toward the door only to pause. "Oh, I forgot to ask, who is your intended?"

"Seth. Seth Nolan."

Bethany could feel her smile become more plastered. "Did you say Seth Nolan?"

Caledonia yawned and nodded. "His letters were so sweet. I'll show them to you one day soon."

"Yes, tomorrow," Bethany murmured and began to close the door. "You rest."

The door clicked closed and her brow furrowed. "Seth Nolan," she whispered as her feet hit the stairway.

All the way down, she pondered over the words from Callie and what she knew as fact. A feeling of dread washed over her as she came to a stop on the first step. "Seth Nolan."

Her eyes focused on the kitchen. Pressing her lips together, her gaze narrowed and she stepped off the stairway.

Crossing her living room, she pushed her sleeves up to the elbows as if preparing for battle. "I think Maxwell and I need to have a little talk."

CHAPTER 5

Max dumped the sack of flour into the bin and sighed. Already, he was getting in deeper than he had planned. Every time he glimpsed that girl, his insides all went funny. "Best thing that could happen would be for me to be killed by lightning."

"What's that?"

Red's voice made him jump. Max turned and found the cowboy standing at the pantry door. He groaned. "I said, we could use a little rain, but not the lightning."

"Yeah." Red rubbed the back of his neck with his right hand. "A might bit humid out there."

Coming out of the small room off of the kitchen, Max closed the door. His eyes spied a box of spices and other small items his mother requested. Still, feeling the need to get his mind in order, he seized on the opportunity. "I'm going to put these things up for Mom. You start getting the feed out of the back and I'll join you."

"Sure thing." Red nodded.

To Max's relief, he sauntered out the door. Heaving a sigh of relief, he moved to the box and began setting the items out on the cutting block. "Got to watch what I'm doing, or the guys are going to think I'm plumb loco," he grumbled.

Still thinking, he didn't hear the soft footsteps of his mother until she spoke.

"Max, there you are."

He jumped and put a hand to his chest. "Ma, you scared me to death."

She gave him a cautionary glare. "Did I? Hmm, perhaps I have a good reason."

Max swallowed. He had a feeling things were going to get worse. "What's the problem?"

"Problem? Perhaps you could tell me."

Immediately, Max felt ten years old again. "Ma'am?"

His mother turned, her face as stern as he had ever seen it. She seemed ready for battle.

He gulped as she crossed to stand in front of

him, and then draw her arms over her chest. He waited, but not for long.

"Did you realize who Miss Caledonia came to marry?"

"I-I..." he paused. The words didn't want to come.

"Maxwell."

The low warning tone had him shuffling in his boots. "Momma," he began and stopped.

There were no words for what he was about to say. Sorry wouldn't cut it. He knew it. His mother would know it. The best thing for him to do would be to come clean. "Momma, it's a bit complicated."

"Oh, Maxwell."

The disappointment in her voice caused him to wither.

"What have you done, son?"

He lifted his hands. "I was only trying to help. When Lou and Teddy spoke to me—" He stopped as she held up her hand.

"I think this will be better with a cup of coffee. You, young man, sit down right over there and get your story straight." His mother moved to the kitchen stove.

Max shuffled his feet across the floor to the kitchen table. Pulling out a handmade chair, he sat down and stared at the grains of wood. If only that table could talk, he mused. He ran his hand along the broad pine boards. Before the ranch was profitable, his father had handcrafted the table for the little cabin that once stood on this spot. His fingers moved over a set of initials carved into the wood.

The pocketknife he had been given for Christmas had been the culprit. Shut in during a January snowstorm, he'd 'practiced' his art. At first, his father had been furious. The knife was confiscated and extra chores added. Yet, his father hadn't sanded them away. It served as a constant reminder of what was expected of a Barringer.

"I've failed again," he murmured.

"Let's not go that far, just yet."

He glanced up as his mother handed him a mug.

"I suggest you start at the beginning."

"The beginning?"

She gave a nod.

"Well, it all began when I saw Lou, Teddy and D.W. go into the saloon without Seth." He explained how the men had written the letters and saved the money to bring Caledonia to Rattlesnake Ridge without Seth's knowledge. "But the kink in their lasso was that Seth went off on business and fell in love."

"Lord, have mercy!" his mother exclaimed. "So, what now?"

Max took a deep breath. "The idea is for me to keep her on the ranch while they raise the money to send her back to Virginia."

He watched his mother shake her head from side to side; as she tried to wrap her mind around all the information he'd laid before her. "You know," she began. "Those three haven't been able to hold on to a nickel if their life depended on it."

"They got her here."

"But, how long did that take?" His mother questioned.

Max voice dropped. "Six months." He glanced over. "But you know Lou and the boys."

Bethany stared at him. "Yes, it could have been even longer."

Both stared at the cups of coffee. "You plan on keeping her here for six months or maybe even year and come up with a different story every time she asks about Seth?"

"No ma'am."

"Max. Max. Max." She sighed heavily. "Well, you're a grown man."

He watched as she got to her feet.

"You are going to have to figure this out for yourself."

"Yes, ma'am."

"But hear me out." She turned to face him. Her finger pointed to the upstairs bedroom where he knew Callie was staying. "That young lady has stored up a lot of hopes and dreams. Her heart will be broken. She's going to feel betrayed, lied too, and made fun of. I don't think she will be one bit happy with any of you." She paused for a breath. "And furthermore, Seth and his new bride will be furious. You may have just lost your best friend."

Listening to her words, Max heart sank.

"I suggest you come up with a plausible explanation for your actions. I think you're going to need it."

"Yes, Ma'am." He stared at the table as his mother left the room.

SHE WASN'T sure how long she'd slept. When Callie opened her eyes a cool breeze and long shadows danced across the floor to greet her. Yawning, she turned and rose from the bed only to stop and gaze out the window at the ranch yard below. Six sleek horses dozed in the corral while just beyond the open barn doors, hands moved to fill a line of wooden buckets up with grain making ready to settle the animals down for the night.

"Apparently, it's later than I think. I wish there were a clock on the wall."

A knock on the door drew her attention. "Yes?"

"Miss Caledonia." A young woman's voice echoed through the wood. "Momma says supper will be ready in just a few minutes, if you'd like to come down."

"Yes, thank you. I'll be down as soon as I freshen up."

She listened as the boot steps faded. Moving to the trunk, she knelt down and flipped the two brass locks on the front. The lid squeaked as she lifted it. Pushing a few things away, she came across a deep emerald green skirt and a white lace blouse. "Yes, perfect. It will be a delight to have something fresh to wear."

Tossing them on the bed, she walked over to the wash stand and was delighted to find the pitcher half filled with water. She lifted the container and poured a generous amount into the bowl. On the rack, a washcloth sat waiting.

"A quick wash up won't take long."

Her fingers worked the buttons on her waist front free. In a few minutes, she had skimmed down to her camisole and petticoats. She plunged the cloth into the bowl and filled it full of lather from the cake of soap. As she brought the rag over her arms, she closed her eyes savoring the feel of skin free from the dust of the trail.

When she finished, she placed the rag over the rack and turned to her clothes. Fully dressed, she paused at the mirror to take a brush to her hair. With her braid secure to the nape of her neck, she opened the door and headed downstairs. She was about to step on the second landing when the sound of voices drifted up to her. Callie paused.

"You've brought home a lot of abandoned things, but this one takes the cake."

A male voice deeper than Max reached her ears.

Oh, yes, Max said he had a brother.

She leaned further hoping to hear more.

A female voice giggled, then spoke. "You remember that scrawny horse Mr. Matheson pawned off on you?"

The male voice snorted. "Told him it was broke to ride, didn't he, Max?"

The girl chuckled again. "How long did it take your leg to heal?"

"Are you two finished?"

Max voice sounded strong and steady. It made her smile.

"As long as Miss McBride is our guest…."

She recognized Mrs. Barringer's voice.

"You two will refrain from this sort of teasing."

"Ah, Momma," the girl whined.

"Melinda."

The tone of her voice was enough to silence her.

"Max is correct. Teasing will not be tolerated in this house."

A small silence followed.

"So, where is this mysterious guest?"

That was her cue. Straightening her shoulders, Callie continued down the stairs.

"I told her we were eating," the girl answered.

Her foot pressed on the last step which gave a slight squeak.

All eyes at the table turned and focused on her.

Her smile trembled. "Sorry, I am late." With her eyes focused on the floor, she crossed the living room to the table.

Chairs scraped the floor as Max and his brother snapped to their feet.

"You are not late at all," Max replied and

stepped to the chair on the right. "Please sit beside Melinda. I'm sure she'll mind her manners."

Callie glanced at the young girl with the bright smile. "I'm sure she will, thank you."

She moved to the chair. Glancing back at Max, she caught his smile and her heart beat a little bit faster. She took her seat and Max moved back to his chair at the end of the table.

Callie pulled the napkin into her lap. "My, this all looks so good."

"I'm sure it's been a while since you've had a good meal,' Bethany murmured.

Caledonia nodded. "Yes, ma'am. I'm very grateful for your hospitality."

Melinda handed her a platter of roast beef. "Momma's best dish," she whispered.

Caledonia took a good slice and passed it to Max. Soon the rest of the bowls followed and her plate was quickly filled.

"I guess I should do the introductions," Max began. "You have met my mother and you have already met my sister."

She turned to her right and with a nod, explained, "I met Melinda when we were coming in." She smiled at the girl beside her. "I was much impressed with your riding skills."

Melinda perked up. "Do you ride?"

Callie shook her head. "I'm afraid back home, our horses were mainly used for farm work. I do remember having a pony as a child."

"What was his name?"

"Her. We called her Snowflake. I enjoyed riding her around the farm. She was a dear little thing."

"Was," Melinda echoed. "What happened to her?"

"Oh, I grew too big and Poppa said we didn't need another mouth to feed with things tight. So, I sold her to a friend down the road for his younger daughter. She's living the life of luxury."

To her surprise, she found Melinda's eyes glistening.

"It must be a very hard thing to do, to sell a part of your heart."

Callie placed her hands in her lap. "It was. But I shall never forget her."

"I'm glad. I don't think I could part at all with Maggie."

"Your horse?"

Melinda nodded. "Augustus gave me Maggie for my birthday."

"Guilty as charged," the other Barringer brother spoke up.

"And across from you," Max drew her attention to his brother. "You have my dear brother, Augustus."

"Please to meet you." She smiled at him.

"Ma'am."

Callie picked up a bit of her meat. Augustus cleared his throat and she looked up.

"What my brother failed to tell you, is that I'm the better looking one."

"Oh, Augustus," Max groaned as his fork clattered to the plate.

Callie's eyes widened and she lowered her fork. She could see that Max's brother enjoyed needling him. "Let me see," she stared at Augustus then Max.

Max's features where strong. His thick blond hair held its own natural curl. He kept it brushed back from his face. She looked over at Bethany. He had his mother's eyes, but not her hair coloring. No, his was similar to Melinda, and must have come from their father.

Augustus was his mother's child. His hair was darker brown and lacked the curl. He too, kept it cut over his ears and parted on the side. The light from the lanterns overhead sent streaks of fire through the layers. But, his looks did not make her insides feel like jelly. He didn't command the room like Max. He was in a league of his own.

"Oh, I don't know." She continued to contemplate the two. "I think this territory has room for both."

Max laughed a deep natural sound that warmed her heart.

"She is too smart for you, Augustus."

"Spoken like King Solomon," he agreed. "Well done, Miss McBride."

"Please, call me Callie."

They began to eat.

"So, what brought you to Rattlesnake Ridge?" Augustus inquired.

"Roll," Max interrupted and thrust a bowl of yeast rolls in front of her.

Callie blinked. "Thank you." She reached for one.

"Ow!" Augustus cried out.

She looked over to see him leaning toward his mother apparently rubbing his shin.

"I think that's enough talk," Bethany replied ignoring her son's plight. "I won't have my supper getting cold."

"Yes, ma'am," Augustus groaned.

Callie broke her roll and noted everyone seemed focused on their meals.

WITH SUPPER COMPLETE; Callie pushed her chair back. "Oh my, that was a wonderful meal. You've cooked Mrs. Barringer, let me do the dishes."

"Certainly, not." Bethany stood.

"Augustus and Melinda can clean the table and help wash. Max, why don't you take Caledonia out on the porch for a bit of air?"

"Are you sure?"

Bethany nodded. "Go, enjoy yourself."

Max stood and moved to her chair holding it so she could stand. "Callie," he whispered.

She turned to find his arm held in a position for her to hold. Her gaze traveled up his arm to his eyes. The depths of brown with gold flecks drew her in deep. For a brief moment, nothing seemed to surround them. She felt safe. Stepping close, she threaded her arm beneath his and smiled back.

His gaze never left her face as he escorted her out the front door.

The cool air seemed to revive her spirits.

Max let go of her arm and she moved to the edge of the porch.

"The air seems so clean, so fresh here." Her eyes remained on the sky. "The heavens seem so full."

Max moved beside her and together they stared at the dark velvet over taking the heavens.

"I feel as if I could reach up and grab a handful of stars."

She heard him chuckle.

"Never quite heard it explained that way, but sure, I'll grab some and put them on your ears, or better yet, set them in your eyes..." His words dwindled.

She stared back at him.

"But you don't need them, do you," he whispered. His eyes searched hers.

Callie felt a strange warmth spiral around her body. The night grew quiet and all she could hear was the sound of his breathing. "That was beautiful," she whispered.

Her voice startled him and he seemed to draw back.

She pulled both hands together and glanced away. "It must be this country."

"Ma'am?"

She looked back and smiled. "It seems to turn every man into a poet."

His brows arched. "My words, or the sky?"

She glanced away. "The sky, of course."

Max shifted his gaze to the heavens and wished he had learned to think before speaking. "Yes, it is."

A bit uncomfortable, she stepped away and moved to the middle of the yard. With slow repetitive speed, she turned in a circle. "Absolutely, worth the trip."

"You think so?"

Callie turned back to look at the house. She watched Max step from the porch and walk toward her. "Yes. I do. I knew it was the right thing to do, to come here to Rattlesnake Ridge. Here, you feel free."

"Free is it?" He drew his arms across his chest and waited for her to finish.

"Yes. I knew once I came here, I'd never want to leave and I'm right. There's so much to do, a home to make, a life to live, a future to bring to life." She waited for him to reply. When no comment came, Callie gave him a shy glance.

Max seemed to study the ground.

"I guess you think I'm silly."

He shook his head. "No, you are not silly at all. I

think anyone would want to stay and follow their dreams."

Callie breathed a sigh of relief. "I look forward to this new adventure. I just can't believe I'm going to marry the man of my dreams, Seth Nolan, and make him proud."

At her words, the light in Max's eyes seemed to fade.

Pain replaced the mirth and an unease over took her. "Max, Is there something I don't know? Something you need to tell me?" She stepped closer and touched his arm. At the warmth of her fingers, the skin beneath his shirt flinched. Dread filled her heart. "Max, Seth is coming, isn't he?" She searched his face. "Max?"

The man before her looked down then glanced back to her.

"He's coming. It will just take a few days, is all."

She felt her world tilt in the right direction. Callie took one more deep breath. "I think I'm going in. It's been a long day and suddenly, I am so tired." She took a few steps toward the house, then paused.

Turning back, she walked to Max and grasping his shoulders, she rose on her tip toes and brushed her lips across his cheek. "Thank you, Max. Thank you for everything."

CHAPTER 6

All the wind went out of his sails. Eyes wide, he watched her walk back to the house and disappeared inside. The right side of his cheek burned as if she'd branded him. Swallowing the thick lump, he reached out and touched his face only to find that she had somehow left no mark.

"Crazy. Just plumb loco," he murmured to no one.

Turning, he moved to the barn. Walking down the center aisle, Max needed to spend some time away from the main house. He needed Callie to turn in before he returned to. One by one, he checked the water for each horse. At the last stall, he turned and gazed at the lights shining through the windows.

"I can't go in the house right now."

"Can't or won't?" The voice in his head questioned.

Ignoring the prick of his subconscious, he picked up a brush and went inside the stall.

The door clicked shut and the horse looked up, questioning his actions.

"Just a good brushing." He turned the brush over in his hand.

The animal snorted and gave a shake of its head, but submitted to the attention without fanfare.

Stroke by stoke, Max brought the brush across the animals fur followed by smoothing it down further with his hand. The horse's deep chestnut coat easily took on a red shine that complimented its flaxen mane.

"Yeah, that's a good girl. You'll be the prettiest filly in the coral come tomorrow."

The horse leaned into the strokes which made Max grin. The repetition of the action allowed the tension in his shoulders to ease.

"You're going to wear the hide off that horse."

Max looked up to see his brother leaning against the post at the horses stall. "Augustus, I didn't hear you come up."

"Nope, you were a bit busy spilling your guts to that animal."

Max turned his attention back to the horse and once again, brought the brush down across her coat.

"You want to tell me what's going on?"

Max paused and pressed his lips together.

"I don't believe for one moment that you did this willingly for Lou, Teddy, and Dill."

A rough breath rushed through Max nostrils. "No. I was tricked."

His answer brought a deep chuckle from his brother. "I'm not surprised. Sometimes, I think those three could sell snake oil to a traveling salesman."

They shared a laugh which eased the tension.

When they paused, Augustus asked. "What's really got under your skin, Max?"

"She's got no business out here," he explained. "She's not strong enough."

"Just that?"

Max gave the horse a pat and she moved away allowing him to walk out of the stall. He didn't speak until he'd put the brush back into the bucket. "That and…."

"And?" Augustus lifted a brow.

"And, she's been lied to and now I've got to figure out a way to get her back home," Max grumbled. "She's just a might of a woman. She shouldn't have to come all the way out here and be disappointed. It's not fair."

"Since when is life ever fair?" Augustus replied. "If it was fair, Pa would still be with us."

Max hung his head. "Yeah, yeah, I know." He drew a breath. "She doesn't seem strong enough to survive in a place like Rattlesnake Ridge."

"Oh, I don't know," Augustus countered. "She was strong enough to survive the trip out here."

"But she had dreams to cling to. What's she gonna do when I tell her they were for nothing?" He paused and stared at the horse.

"Speaking of that, how did she get here?"

"False pretenses," Max grudgingly admitted. "If I could get a hold of Lou, Teddy, and Dill, I'd give 'em a good thrashing." As he explained, his brother's eyes widened. "Now they've gone and got me mixed up in this – this thing." Max glanced away before he confessed, "I'm in deep, Augustus. So deep, I don't know how to climb out."

Silence slid between the two brothers.

"I don't know what to tell you?"

Max shrugged. "Not much to tell. If I were a

man, I'd march right in that house and tell her the whole sorted truth."

Augustus glanced over his shoulder at the open barn door. "I don't think that's a good idea tonight. She's tired. You need some time to think of how to handle this and not get anyone killed, especially yourself."

Neither spoke as the horse moved away signaling to the men it wanted to go to sleep.

"I guess we've kept this horse up too long." Max sighed.

"I'll leave you to finish up and close the door. Oh, Max?"

"Yeah?" he turned to face his brother.

"Don't worry, if anyone can figure a way out of this, it will be you."

Max snorted. "Tell that to the sheriff when she has me arrested."

Augustus broke into a wide grin. "Naw, I'm gonna put it on your tombstone." He swiped the air with his hand. "Here lies, Maxwell Barringer, killed by love."

Max shoved his brother away from him. "Go on to the house with you. Melinda's probably waiting with a chess game."

His brother winced. "She probably is. You sure you don't want to play against her?"

"No one female is enough to deal with."

His brother's smile faded. "You will be all right, won't you, Max?"

"Yeah, I'll be fine," he lied. "Go on."

With no other alternative, Augustus left the barn.

Max made one last visual check before he walked out into the night. The shadows along the open ground had deepened to ebony. Hidden by the darkness, the crickets serenaded their mates and answering chorus filled the night air.

"No use hiding out here," Max grumbled.

Hands shoved deep in his pockets and shoulders hunched nearly to his earlobes, he made his way back to the house. He paused at the door. His thumb pressed the metal latch.

"Be brave," he told himself and shoved the door wide.

Warm air flowed past him seeking to disappear into the night. Across the room, he spied his mother with her basket of darning. She glanced up from the tedious work.

He refused to meet her gaze.

"Close the door, Max."

"Yes, ma'am."

Door closed, Max spied his brother Augustus locked in a game of chess with Melinda. He gazed over his sister's head. His face bore that 'I told you so look'.

"Everything all right out at the barn?" His mother questioned. "You were gone so long, I was beginning to worry."

"Yes, ma'am, everything is fine. I just checked water." Max ignored the curious look from his sister. Walking to a shelf along the far wall, he grabbed a book and ambled over to the chair next to the fireplace. Blowing out a deep breath, he sat down and absentmindedly flipped the cover open. Words in black type filled the page, but none of them made sense. To be honest, he didn't really care. He was holding a book and to the world, he was occupied. To the world, he was busy. Max, however, was using the time to try and sort out the jumble of feelings that ate at his soul.

The wood crackled in the hearth as the flames licked at the logs.

"Caledonia went to bed," Melinda informed him. "She said she was tired."

Max glanced up and watched her move a pawn. "Expect she was," he answered and flipped a page.

Out of the corner of his eye, he watched his sister narrow her eyes. Nope, he wasn't rising to the bait. If Melinda wanted to tease him, she was going to have to find something better than that.

"Come on, Mel. Your turn," Augustus grumbled as he drew her back to the board.

With a huff, his sister turned in her chair and looked back down at her last move.

Max gave his attention to the letters on the page. Instead of reading, his mind tried to make sense of everything that went on today.

Dang it, she was in love with Seth and he'd gone and married another. It was sure some kind of mess to fall into his lap. He'd seen a woman angry – once. One of the sodbusters had gotten a snoot full at Dobson's saloon. His wife had marched right in and took a swipe at his head with a big ole cast iron frying pan. Max gave a shiver. Callie couldn't pick up one of those let alone swing it. Still, the notion of her anger made him want to slink under the steps like dog getting a tongue lashing.

There would be a bucket or two of tears shed once she found out that Seth had already married. Perhaps, he could step into the fray and remind her that men just can't control their feelings. Seth didn't mean to get married; it was thing that just sort of happened. No, he couldn't do that. First of all, Seth would not be pleased. He'd be nothing more than a low life playing on her heartache. Second, it wasn't the truth. He needed a better story.

He raised his hand and leaned an elbow on the arm of his chair, before nestling his chin against his palm. She was brought out here with lies, no matter how good they were intended, and that alone, would break her heart even if Dill, Teddy, and Lou put hat to hand and confessed. The truth made him squirm in the chair causing it to squeak.

His mother sighed and put down her work once again. "Max, you act as if something's bothering you?" He looked over the binding of the book. "No, I'm fine."

He was as long as he didn't have to tell the truth. That would hurt too much. The mental image of those blue eyes mired in tears seemed to open a wound he couldn't heal. He stared at the paper. A story, he needed a good story that would satisfy her inquisitive nature and keep her from being inconsolable.

"One that might save my hide as well as theirs," he mumbled under his breath.

"Did you say something, Max?"

Augustus voice made him jerk his head up and

shift his glance from side to side. *Had he spoke aloud?* The questioning glance on Melinda's face and the all too knowing one on his mother's confirmed his suspicions. "Sorry, thinking about a problem Cameron told me about."

"Hopefully, the equipment you had to get from Carson City will ease that problem," his mother replied as she pulled her thread through the seam.

"Yep, I'm sure Carson City had a lot to do with it." Augustus lips twitched as he moved a white chess piece.

Max refused to answer.

But his mother's blistering glare silenced his brother for two more moves on the chess board.

"Checkmate, Mel." He placed his queen before her king. "Ah, Augustus," she groaned.

"Study a bit more," he remarked. Leaving his little sister to study the board, he stood and made his way over to the hearth. Lifting his foot, he placed a boot on the stone and grabbed the poker. Augustus leaned forward and shifted the log toward the back, stirring up a shower of sparks as the log broke in two. Without turning his head, he lowered his voice so only Max could hear, "That load you're carrying seems mighty heavy, brother."

NAN O'BERRY

Max lifted his gaze and watched the yellow light shimmer along his brother's face.

Augustus turned and looked at him. "You need help…." He let the sentence hang.

"I'll manage."

"Yep, right." The tone of Augustus voice signaled he didn't believe him. Instead of pointing out the obvious, he asked another question, "Are you heading up to meet with Cameron at the logging camp tomorrow?"

"Got to go," Max replied. "Supplies are needed. Cameron will be looking for that block and tackle to help get the logs on the flume to send down to the mill. Winthrop has a big project in the works."

Augustus gave a grunt. "When doesn't he?"

"You'll be okay till I get back?"

Augustus nodded. "I've got a few horses to begin to gentle."

"How's the south pasture look? Is it ready for cutting?"

"It will be in a few weeks. Looks like a good crop."

The two grew silent.

"Your friend," Augustus began. "Will she be staying here, at the ranch?"

"I got no place for her to go. She can't go in

town alone. If she struck up a conversation, you know what would happen."

Augustus took a deep breath. "Seth would find out in a heartbeat."

Max nodded.

"He back in town?"

"According to Lou, yes, but he and his new bride are getting to know one another."

His brother's cheeks turned red and he gave a cough. "I bet."

Max pressed his lips together in a thin line. "Watch yourself, little brother. I'm not in a forgiving mood."

Augustus held his hand up. "No offense meant." He brought his leg down and stepped back from the hearth. "I think I'm going to bed. I hope you're able to sleep tonight. That's a lot of information to juggle."

Max noted he punctuated his statement with a large yawn.

"You enjoy your book. He moved away and headed toward the stairs. "Oh and Max?"

"Yeah?"

"Since when did you get some interested in Fairy Tales?"

Max blinked. He glanced down at the book he

was holding. The spine had gold embossed letters that read, 'Grimm's Fairy Tales'.

"Hey, that's mine," Melinda groaned and moving to his chair took it from his hands. "Get your own book!"

"Sorry, thought it was Plutarch." Max slunk down in the seat as Augustus laughter filtered down from the stairway.

CALLIE DIDN'T WANT to open her eyes. It had been way too long since she had the luxury of clean sheets. She breathed deep and stretched. Oh, she should be up, helping Mrs. Barringer with the chores, but...

"Just a little while longer," she murmured.

Last night, she'd left the front window of her room cracked despite the cold. Now, she could hear the chirp of the song birds and the voices of the cowboys that worked on the Diamond B.

"Get those horses watered." Augustus' voice called out.

She remembered that Max said five men helped his younger brother. A male voice answered but it was too far away for her to make out the exact words. A horse neighed. Somewhere in the distance, a rooster crowed.

Callie opened her eyes and stared at the ceiling. "So, this is what it's like to wake up to ranch life," she mused. "Not so much different than our farm."

She pulled her arms from beneath the blankets and crossed them over her chest. Below her, the heavy door to the house opened and slammed shut. The sound of boots running off the porch and onto the gravel in front of the house followed

"Slow down, Mel," Augustus called out.

"Got to get the eggs."

"Watch those horses."

Another neigh followed.

The banter between the two made her smile. "I hope when Seth and I have children, they will be that close."

She breathed deep once more before throwing back the covers and to rise. Moving to the window, she leaned against the opening and looked out on to the scene below. Two cowboys were carrying buckets of water to the troughs in the corral. She could see Max and his brother working to pull the wagon she'd ridden in on out from under the shelter next to the barn.

Once in the clear, she watched Max disappear

into the barn while Augustus waited. Minutes later, he led the two horses out and together they backed the animals so the wagon tongue was between them.

"That's right. Max has equipment to deliver to the lumber camp."

Augustus looked up. He smiled as he straightened and lifted a hand. "Good Morning." His voice rang out across the barnyard. Max turned around and looked up at her window.

Callie realized she had been caught spying. "Morning," she called back.

Max stepped away from the wagon and moved toward the house. "Did you sleep well?"

She nodded. "Best sleep I've had in weeks."

"There's coffee in the kitchen. Breakfast will be ready in few minutes."

"I'll be right down." Moving away from the window, Callie hurried to pull out some fresh clothing. The water in the pitcher was cool but it would have to do. Washing her face, she donned her skirt and blouse before sending a brush through her hair. Pulling it toward the top of her head, she gave a few twists and used her hair pins to capture it in place. Her high top boots laced, she opened her door and headed down to the first floor.

At the landing, she could hear the bang of the

door on the cast iron stove swing shut. Walking around to the archway, she spied Max's mother moving back to the chopping block and the side of bacon waiting to be slice. "Can I help?"

Bethany looked up. "You sure you want to? You are our guest."

"I'm positive."

"Apron's hanging the peg. There are eggs in the bowl that need to be scrambled."

Callie donned the white muslin and moved to the bowl on the counter. Six brown eggs lay in the bottom and a glass of milk beside it. She wiped her hands on the towel lying next to it and then reached in to grasp the chicken's offerings. One by one, she tapped the eggs against the lip of the bowl and emptied the contents. Pouring the milk into the mix, she added a dash of salt and pepper before picking up the whisk and whipping the ingredients together. Working in tandem, the two soon had the meal ready for the table. Callie was pouring coffee into the cups as the door opened and Max entered.

She put the pot down and smiled. "Morning."

"Morning," he answered.

They stared at each other. She tried to think of something to say. "You-you are going to the lumber camp today?"

He nodded. "Got to deliver the supplies." He gave a jerk of his thumb in the direction of the front door and the wagon waiting outside.

"It will be a nice day for a journey." She smiled at him.

His grin widened. "Yes, it will."

"Oh, Max," his mother interrupted. "Call Augustus and Melinda, breakfast is ready."

"Yes, ma'am." Max hurried out the door.

As a loud bell rang, Mrs. Barringer entered from the kitchen with a platter of biscuits piled high.

"Let me put this towel down," Callie folded the towel in her hand and placed it on an empty spot in the middle of the table.

"Thank you, dear."

The scuffle of feet on the wood floor gave notice that the others had arrived.

"Did you get the eggs, Melinda?"

"Yes, ma'am." The young girl held up a basket containing several.

"Put them in the kitchen. We'll wash them after we eat."

Callie watched as Mrs. Barringer moved to the head of the table. Max hurried over and pulled the chair out for his mother.

"Thank you."

Then, he moved to the chair beside Callie. She watched as his hands grasped the chair and pulled it out for her. A rush of heat pooled in her cheeks. She tipped her chin forward and whispered, "Thank you," as she took her seat.

They waited for Melinda to return from the kitchen and take her seat.

Then, Max and Augustus joined them.

"Shall we hold hands?"

Callie reached out with her right hand and grasped Mrs. Barringer's. Holding out her left hand, she felt Max's calloused palm take hers. A jolt of warmth just like the day before shot up her arm and made her heart beat erratically.

"Let us bow our heads," Bethany said.

Please, don't let anyone at the table notice the way I shiver. She prayed silently.

"Heavenly Father, thank You for allowing us another day in Your beautiful world. Keep our family safe as they go about their daily chores and bring them back home again."

Callie felt Mrs. Barringer squeeze her fingers.

"Thank You, Lord, for bringing Miss Caledonia McBride into our lives. We hope You will make her new life here in Rattlesnake Ridge all that she imagined. Amen."

"Amen," they all answered.

Callie opened her eyes surprise to find them shinning with tears. "Thank you," she murmured to Max's mother.

Bethany Barringer gave her a wink.

CHAPTER 7

Max tapped the rump of the chestnut gelding with the leather reins as he rounded the curve and headed up the grade to the logging camp. The morning light had just crested the hills and streaked the land with its golden rays as it continued to rise into the sky. Glancing up, he yawned.

"Could have used a couple more hours of sleep," he grumbled to no one.

The horse snorted.

Max pressed his lips into a thin line. He knew all too well what prevented his good night's sleep.

"That woman," he muttered.

His dreams magnified the touch of her hand the

soft brush of her lips against his cheek, and the soft fresh scent that was totally female.

"How did she get under my skin so fast?"

He gave a shake of his head. He'd given up all pretenses and risen before the sun, hitched up the wagon, and met his mother coming down the stairs as he was going out to get the wagon ready. Once they'd finished breakfast, he'd hurried out of the yard as if Satan was at his heels. If she thought it strange, she didn't say and he didn't wait around for any discussion to uncover his motives.

The horse leaned against its yoke and the wagon groaned as it slowed.

"Come on, Jake. Get up."

The animal pressed forward and soon the wagon drew to the crest.

"Whoa," Max called. His foot on the brake, he pulled back on the reins, and brought the animal to a halt.

The horse blew out a deep breath and gave a toss of his head.

"Let's get our breath before we head into the camp."

Climbing down from the wagon, Max grabbed the canteen and walked toward the animal. Unscrewing the top, he poured a little water into his hand and allowed the horse to drink. When Jake was satisfied, he placed the cap back on and moved back to the wagon. Hesitating, he took time to glance around the hillside. The slopes above Lake Tahoe were dotted with huge ponderosa pines and hardwoods. The contrast from the dark earth to the deep green seemed comforting to the eye.

"God's country, full of promises."

Yeah, he could understand why Callie took the opportunity to come out. He placed the canteen back in the box and leaned his arms over the side. He wasn't in any real hurry to climb back on.

"Maybe I ought to check out those letters in the General Store to see why women come out here. Perhaps, I can figure a story to help ease the shock."

As soon as he said it, Max hung his head.

"Nope, I need to tell her the truth." He looked up and watched a doe race across the hillside below him. "She's not going to believe it. I'm not even sure I believe it."

He grabbed the side of the wagon and lifted his body back to the seat.

"Something will come to me, it always does." Max picked up the reins. "Come on Jake, let's get to the camp before Cameron wonders what's up."

Releasing the brake with his foot, Max gave

Jake his head and the horse leaned into his collar moving the wagon toward the lumber camp high on Rattlesnake Ridge.

CALLIE PULLED the rag across the top of the table behind the sofa and hummed to herself. Her heart had been disappointed when she learned Max had departed shortly before breakfast.

"I guess he had to go to work. I just wish he could have stayed to show me around a bit."

She gave a sigh and picked up the glass vase to capture the dust hiding beneath. Setting it back down, she gave a gentle touch to the prisms that hung around the base of the globe. A stream of light burst into the colors of the rainbow. She stepped back and watched the light dance across the room.

"Oh, my."

Caught off guard by the unexpected voice, she took two quick steps back from the table. Her eyes widened as she glanced over at the dining room where Mrs. Barringer stood. "I didn't mean…."

Bethany waved away her explanation. "Oh, not to worry, I'm very used to Melinda doing the same thing as she comes in every day." She walked to the end of the table and placed her hands on her hips. "I really must thank you for offering to do the dusting. Melinda attention span is – well." She shrugged. "My daughter loves the outdoors."

Callie returned the smile. "It's not a problem. I enjoy keeping busy."

Bethany smiled. "I was hoping you would say that. Put that away and come over here. I've been working on selecting quilt colors and I need a pair of fresh eyes."

"Of, course. Happy to be of help." Placing the rag in the wooden box on the chair near the sofa, Callie hoisted it against her hip and moved toward the table.

"The light is better in here," Bethany explained drawing Callie's attention to the line of windows along the back wall. "I like to see how my cloth looks. You know my eyes aren't as good as they used to be. Just put the box on the edge there."

Callie joined in her chuckle as she placed the box on the edge before moving next to her. "Oh, I love that purple." Reaching out, she ran her fingers over the smooth cotton print.

"It is pretty isn't it? Melinda loves that color."

"Does Melinda help you quilt?"

Max's mother took a deep breath. "I had hoped Melinda would help me make it."

"I take it, she's not a quilter?"

Bethany gazed over at her and raised a bow. "Not in the slightest." She glanced around the empty house. "You see, she has already found another place to be, no doubt, following behind her brother."

Callie tried to hide the smile on her face. She placed a sympathetic hand on the woman's shoulder. "It's going to be just fine. We'll make it for her. What pattern are you doing?" Callie caught the growing smile on Bethany's face. She felt her hand touch her arm.

"I'm so glad you are here. I was just feeling a bit defeated. I'll get the pattern." Bethany moved to the sideboard on the wall behind them.

Bethany left her alone; Callie began to move the pieces of fabric around finding a pleasing pattern.

"I've been saving all the newspaper the boys bring home to cut out my pattern pieces," Bethany spoke aloud. "Ah, here."

Callie looked over to the right as she placed a metal tin on the table and pulled the lid off.

"Bear paw," Bethany said with glee, as she placed the well folded piece of paper on the table. "I love this pattern."

For the next hour, the two cut out pieces and placed them in the sewing basket.

Finally, Bethany put down the scissors and took a deep sigh. "Let's get a cold glass of water and move to the front porch."

Following Bethany into the kitchen, she waited while she poured two glasses of cold water. "Thank you." Callie murmured as she took the glass.

"Let's go enjoy the sunshine."

With Max's mother leading the way, they moved out onto the covered porch.

"Over here," Bethany called and led her to a small table set up to the left of the front door.

Sitting down, they both stared at the activity in the barnyard. One of the hands was busy raking the straw from the barn, while a second had a saddle thrown over a wooden barrel and appeared to be mending some of the leather. A neigh from the corral drew Callie's attention.

"Take it easy with her," Melinda called out from her perch on the top rail of the fence.

"What are they doing?" Callie asked.

"Oh, Augustus wants to begin training a new filly. Melinda adores horses," Bethany answered.

"Augustus doesn't let her work with the horses?"

Bethany shook her head. "He's afraid she might

get hurt. He'll let Hank work with her until she's used to the halter, then Melinda will be allowed to help."

They watched a few more minutes as the wrangler began to teach the young horse to follow his lead as they walked around the corral.

"Tell me, Mrs. Barringer," Callie began.

"Bethany, remember."

Callie smiled. "Tell me; was it hard for you in the beginning?"

"Hard?" Max's mother turned with a quizzical expression etched in her face. "I'm not sure I'm following you."

Callie dampened her lips before she began once more, "Was it hard for you to begin here, begin a new life?" When there was no answer, Callie glanced down at the hem of her skirts. "I've no one else to ask," she admitted. "My mother passed when I was merely five. My father and our housekeeper raised me through the war. I – I," she could feel the heat crawl up her neck and settle in her cheeks. Turning to study the woman beside her, she asked. "I guess, I need to know if I am up to the task?"

To her surprise, a soft chuckle rose from Bethany's lips. "My dear, Caledonia, any woman who gathered her courage to travel all the way from

Virginia on nothing more than a promise to marry sight unseen, is brave enough to conquer the world."

Callie looked away. "What if I fail," she questioned.

"Every woman I know fears failure," Bethany explained. Leaning back, a sigh escape her lips. "When I first came here, there were only a few shacks in town that really didn't appear in habitable. The mines had failed. The town of Rattlesnake Ridge barely existed. We had to go to Reno or Carson City for supplies. And here I was expecting a child and barely able to help my husband. No doctor. The thought of giving birth without assistance gave me more than one or two sleepless nights."

"What did you do?"

"I thought my husband had lost his mind at first. But he was so determined. He filed a claim on the land here and slowly began to cut the trees and build our home while working for Winthrop."

"But you did make it," Callie asserted.

"Yes, we did," Bethany shook her head. "Not without our share of tears and heartache. With good friends we brought Max into this world. We focused and worked together. Just as the ranch was coming into its own, my husband Duncan was killed in a roundup. I thought my world had ended."

"Oh, I'm so sorry," Callie whispered. "I shouldn't have brought this up."

Bethany reached over and grasped Callie's hand. "It's fine. If your mother were here, she'd tell you all good things come with a bit of pain. I'm so proud of all of my children. Their loss made them grow closer together. They understand what family means." She cocked her head. "If I were your mother, I'd tell you as you begin your life as a wife, ask yourself what are your beliefs? Where are your feet grounded?"

Callie grew somber listening to the questions.

"When Melinda's time comes to leave the house and begin her life, I'd tell her this; God made Eve from Adam's rib, not from his behind. A woman's place is not walking behind her man, but beside him. She is his helpmate. A man who is worthy of her, will adore her and hold her in the highest esteem. You work together. Your struggles will become his struggles and in turn, his struggles will become yours. Never stop talking or dreaming. Never go to bed before telling each other that you love them. The key is the word, together."

Tears sprang into Callie's eyes as Bethany's words touched her. "Thank you, Bethany. I will cherish those words and do my best to live up to them."

With a gentle squeeze, Bethany nodded. "Then you will do well."

MAX ROUNDED the trail by the lake and the sound of axes biting deep into wood reached his ears. A familiar smell of pine and wood smoke drifted just about the tree tops reminding him he was almost there. The rumble in the emptiness of his stomach reminded him that he'd left before grabbing a bite to eat.

"Hurry, Jake, I could use a good cup of coffee and one of Sawdust's biscuits about now."

The horse flicked his ears and pulled at the reins as his feet picked up the pace. The tree line slid away and out of the wilderness a broad meadow spread across the mountain side. Logs in various stages of evolution transformed the landscape on the southern side of the hill. Up on the north face, tents that house lumberjacks while they were on the mountain littered the clearing.

The sound of the wagon drew attention from a group that was working on removing the limbs from a good sized pine. A logger put down his end of the two-man saw and called out, "Max!"

Max lifted a hand as he moved passed.

"Cameron is sure going to be glad to see you."

Max laughed. "Cook got a good lunch today? I'd hate to have to go home for a bite to eat."

The logger laughed. "Got some fresh stew and plenty of hot coffee."

"Sounds good." Max nodded.

A wave of his hand and the young man hurried back to his work.

Down at the far end of the encampment, a lone yellow clapboard cabin stood beside a longer pole cabin made from rough hewn logs. A pipe belched smoke into the sky and beside the door a pole with a metal triangle stood ready to call the men in for their hot meal of the day. Pulling past the kitchen, Max stopped his wagon at the yellow cabin as a tall figure in a white button shirt stepped out.

Cameron Cash rolled the ends of his cuffs back down to and buttoned them at his wrists. "Max, I'm glad to see you."

"Whoa there, Jake. Howdy, Cameron," he began as the wagon drew to a stop. He wrapped the reins around the brake and hopped down.

"Thought you'd be here sooner." Cameron

stepped around the horse's head and extended his hand.

Max took it and they shook. "Would have been here sooner but ran into a bit of trouble."

Immediately, the head of Winthrop Timber's face became etched with concern. "Family okay?"

Max nodded. "Yes, they're all fine. Didn't get back until late. Ran into Lou, Dill and Teddy in Carson City…."

Cameron held up his hand. "You needn't explain any more. Those three could talk the horns off a Billy goat and still not make sense."

"You don't know how right you are," Max echoed beneath his breath.

"Did you get those blocks?"

"Yes, they came in." Max reached into the pocket of his trousers and brought out a folded manifest which he handed to his boss. "There are six crates, four sets in each." He pointed over to the back of the wagon. "Three heavy duty ropes and several new blades. You will have to send someone back for the engine to replace the one in the sawmill." He pointed at the invoice. "Says, it will be in two weeks from tomorrow."

"Good. Good," he mumbled.

Max stood back and allowed Cameron to cross

in front of him, then he fell in line behind as they walked over to the rear of the wagon.

"Here take this."

Max reached for the papers Cameron handed him. He watched as his boss tossed back the tarp to get a visual accounting. He noticed the change in his boss's composure. The careful concentration slipped from his features, to be replaced by intense astonishment.

Max asked, "Is something wrong?"

Cameron gave him a speculative gaze that made Max's heart pound. "What?"

Without answering, Cameron leaned over and reached between two crates. His hand closed around something and Max craned his head to see if he could discern the problem.

"What's this?"

Max swallowed as Cameron turned his hand over and slowly exposed the object one finger at a time.

His eyes bulged at the tiny purple satin ribbon rosette nestled in the palm of his boss's hand.

Cameron's brows adjusted high on his forehead as his expression questioned Max. "That must have been some trouble."

Max gaze felt his jaw go slack. No words came

as he tried to explain, "I – I," he began. Yet, no words followed. He looked back to Cameron whose eyes seemed filled with mirth.

"I think, I'd like to hear about this bit of trouble. You unload the wagon and I will meet you over at Cookie's."

Shoulders slumped, Max walked to Jake's head. From behind him, he could hear Cameron deep chuckle as he moved away.

"Lou, Dill, and Teddy owe me big time."

CAMERON SAT BACK and stared at Max. "You are joking…right?"

Max stared his friend and boss, then began the slow shake of his head.

Cameron leaned closer to the table. His hands wrapped around each side of the mug. "You have to tell her."

Max took a deep breath."I know. I came up here hoping to find the answer. I have five days before I head back down to the ranch. Five days to come up with some plausible reason."

"It sounds like you're grasping at straws."

Max snorted and ran his hand through his hair.

"Because, I am." He gave a shake of his head. "Lou said it was best for me to take her to the ranch because Mother and Melinda would be there."

"But?"

"The suggestion seemed like a good one." Max scratched his head. "I mean it seemed a good thing at the time. I had to tell Mother and then, Augustus. They're doing what they can to help."

"So what are you worried about?"

Max glanced over the table. "What if someone comes from town?"

"You expecting anyone?"

Max shook his head. "But some of them church women might come out to get Mother's help for the church. I'd hate for Miss Brown to find out."

Cameron grew thoughtful. "Or worse, Mrs. Handley."

Both men exchanged glances.

"You don't think I could get arrested for helping them do you? Winthrop doesn't take any mess and neither does the sheriff."

Cameron took a breath. "I-I don't think so. I suppose your mother will keep her busy." Max nodded. "She promised me she would. I feel the longer she stays the more likely we are to run out of excuses for taking her into town. I just gotta keep her hidden until Lou and the boys get their money straight."

"Yes," Cameron mused.

The sounds of boots sliding to a stop made them both look up.

"Sorry, Boss, can we borrow Max?" Chip asked as he pulled the red cap from his head. "We got the ropes untangled at the log flume."

"Sure."Max pushed his cup to the center of the table as he rose.

"Let me know what you come up with," Cameron said. "I'm curious to hear of the outcome."

"You and me both," Max grumbled as he left the building with Chip at his side.

They headed across the camp to where the huge wooden structure stood.

"So what's going on? You got trouble?" Chip asked, bouncing along beside Max.

Max pressed his lips together. "You said you had problems over at the flume."

"Oh, we do. We do. Ropes got twisted and the log jerked. Me and the boys have the ropes untangled, but we need an extra pair of hands to thread the rope in the block."

"What about the log?"

"Got it resting on the flume. You really got lady problems?"

"Let it ride, Chip. Let's concentrate on the problems at hand."

"But—"

"Chip."

The warning tone in Max's voice silenced the young logger.

Pushing through the brush, Max could see several of the loggers were gathered around the block and tackle held aloft by three poles. The log sat one end on the flume, the other on the ground, its tip buried a few inches in the rich, dark earth. "You didn't tell me part of it was skewered in the dirt."

Chip shrugged and stuck his hands in his pants pocket.

"Going to take half a day to get this cleaned up," Max muttered beneath his breath. "No one hurt?"

"No, just the rope tangled and snapped," another logger spoke.

"So I see." Max marched toward the group and they parted like the waves before the bow of a ship.

"It wasn't our fault, Max. The darn rope got twisted when we was hauling it up."

Max looked to his left. "And you didn't stop to untangle it?"

The logger stared at his feet. "We were trying to hurry. I guess you can say we weren't really paying attention."

"Yeah, I see." Grasping the dangling rope, Max gazed up at the wooden block and the ropes hanging slack. "Go to the supply house and bring me some of that new cable I brought back." He looked around at the crowd. "Sam, you give me a hand and we'll get this wrapping off. Ox, you and three more stay and help hold the log once we get this rethreaded. The rest of you log jockeys get back to work. Trees don't fell themselves."

Grumbling, the men dispersed.

"All right." Max pulled his gloves from his back pocket. "Let's get this fixed. I got some things to do at home."

CHAPTER 8

*A*ugustus wiped his shirtsleeve across his brow as he entered the living room of the Barringer cabin. "I think Max knew it was going to turn hot," he grumbled as he tossed his hat onto the table by the door.

"Hang your hat up. I've put some fresh towels and water on the porch. You wash up before you come to my table," Bethany ordered.

Grumbling, Augustus turned on his heel and hurried outside.

Callie entered carrying the platter of fried chicken, her cheeks ruddy red from the heat that seemed to be building all day long.

Bethany pushed her sleeves up her arms. "Put the platter in the center. I must admit, Augustus might be right. It has to be cooler up on the mountain rather than here in the valley."

The sounds of boots at the door turned both their heads.

"I'm going up to get a fresh shirt," Augustus announced.

"Send Melinda down will you? I sent her upstairs to clean up as well."

With a nod, her youngest son went three steps up before yelling, "MEL, MOM NEEDS THE TABLE SET."

Bethany cringed and then muttered, "You'd think they were all raised in a barn."

Her annoyance made Callie giggle.

Her infectious laugh brought a smile to Bethany's face. "Honest, I did raise them proper."

"I bet you did."

Melinda's hurried steps pounded down steps.

Callie was delighted to see her wearing a soft sage colored skirt and off-white blouse.

Her face had been scrubbed and her ponytail redone. "Sorry." She reached for the plate, Callie held out for her.

Between the two, the table was set and ready by the time Augustus rejoined them.

"Come, let's take a seat and eat. Then we can go outside for a bit. It has to be cooler than inside."

Augustus offered to hold the chair for each of the ladies before taking his seat.

"Caledonia, will you say grace this evening?" Bethany inquired.

"Of course."

Hands joined around the table and heads bowed, Callie spoke, "Dear Lord, we thank You for a wonderful day. I've had the pleasure of learning so much about Your great wilderness. Look down upon this wonderful family and shed Your grace upon them as they go about their chores. In Your name, we pray."

"Amen."

The sound of a familiar male voice caused Callie's eyes opened wide. The grasp of hands at the table fell away. Pushing back her chair, Callie drew her gaze to the door and watched as Max, hat in hand, strode through the opening. There was no ignoring the focus of his gaze.

"You came home," she whispered.

His smile grew as he stepped inside. "I guess I couldn't miss my Mother's cooking."

"I-I see." Her voice was breathless.

"Max," Bethany spoke. Her voiced sounded a

bit bemused. "We didn't expect you back this evening."

"We finished up early, Cameron said, he'd call me if he needed any more help." His gaze shifted momentarily away from Callie. "Do you have enough for one more?"

"Of course we do." His mother chuckled. "Melinda will set you a place right beside Caledonia?"

Max focused once again on her and she smiled softly before lowering her gaze. He was staring at her with those deep intense eyes. Eyes that made her heart pound against her ribs. Lord, it was getting quite warm in the house. She wished for a fan to brush the breeze across her skin to take away the heat.

"Momma," Melinda started to wail, but her mother's quick glance silenced the young girl.

"Well, if it's okay, I'll run upstairs and clean up," Max said.

"By all means."

Callie was surprised to find her heart racing. His boots echoed against the wood as he made his way toward the stairs. Cautiously, she shifted her gaze and watched him bound up the stairway to the second floor.

A chair across the table squeaked as it was drawn back.

"How nice that Max could make it home," Melinda murmured as she rose. "Usually, he stays up at the logging camp for a day or two."

"Yes, how nice," Callie murmured.

"Melinda, go get the plate, dear, Max will be down very soon."

"Yes, Momma."

Hearing the Max's sister move away, Callie lifted her gaze. She found three pair of eyes studying her. Flustered, she fumbled with her napkin and drew it into her lap.

"Go on, Melinda," Bethany whispered.

CALLIE FOUND that with Max sitting next to her, her appetite fled. She listened to the conversation and teasing around her. The laughter relaxed her, yet the nearness of the man next to her seems almost, overwhelming.

"Caledonia, do you prefer something else?" Bethany inquired. "You've barely eaten at all."

She glanced over at the concern on Bethany's face. "No, the chicken is wonderful. I'm just enjoying the company."

"Ah. Well, I think I'm going to begin cleaning up. Augustus, Melinda, lets clear the table and get the dishes done." Rising, Bethany Barringer picked up the dishcloth and fashioned it around the handle of the coffee pot.

"Lucky you," Augustus hissed over the table as he gathered his plate and utensils.

Max kept his eyes focused on his plate but Callie caught the impish smile that flashed the dimples that surrounded his lips. "You seem rather smug."

Max lifted his head and gave her a wide-eyed innocent glance. "What? Me?" His lips twitched. "Innocent as a newborn lamb."

Callie shook her head.

"Don't believe me?"

"No." She lifted her hand in her defense. "I didn't say that."

Max rested his forearms on the edge of the table. His grin widened. "You're a smart girl then."

Callie put down her fork. "I declare it is just too warm to eat."

"Yes." Max pulled the napkin from his lap and placed it over his plate. "Shall we take a walk?"

"I'd like that."

Max pushed his chair back and rose from the

table. He grasped the back of the chair and eased it from the table allowing her to stand.

"Thank you." She placed her knife and fork on the plate. "Should we take them to the kitchen?"

"No. Let Melinda take care of that. Come on." His hand resting comfortably at her back, Max led her outside to the cool breeze that pushed the heat away from the house, under the overhang of the porch.

Callie walked to the edge of the porch and placed a hand on the stout column that was once a pine tree. "My, it's beautiful."

"That it is. I don't think I could imagine myself living anywhere else," Max answered.

"The other day, you said you came here as a child. How old were you?"

"Oh, I think I was about twelve. Augustus was eight and Miss Mel, she was no more than a year old."

"That must have been an undertaking."

Max moved to the other side of the stout post and leaned his shoulder against the wood. "It was the best of times. I worked side by side with my dad, helping to put this house together. I couldn't do a lot of the heavy lifting, but Pa hired some of the hands from the nearby ranches to do the heavy beams."

"He picked the right spot for this house."

Max nodded. "He walked around and around, noting the sunrise and sunset for nearly two weeks before he placed the cornerstones." He pushed away from the post. "Come with me." He held out a hand.

Callie looked at the open palm.

"Come, I want to show you something. The other day, you saw the night in the farm yard. I want to show you my father's favorite place."

With a smile, she placed her hand in his. The warmth of contact was now becoming familiar. Yet, it didn't stop the heat from swirling to her cheeks.

Max led her off the porch and down a path that moved away from the main structure and led down toward the west.

There wasn't much conversation as they moved along the tall stately pines that shaded their path. It widened to a small opened area that over looked the valley below. To the west, the tall mountain peaks of the Sierra Nevada Range loomed. Each cragged peak bathed in a golden glow of the setting sun.

"Oh, Max," Callie whispered in wonder.

"Come over here and sit." He led her to a long flat stone that seemed to be placed at the center of the opening just for watching the evening begin.

Using his hand, Max brushed off the dirt and pine needles.

Callie took her seat while Max joined her.

They didn't speak. They didn't have to. The beauty of the moment was too much for words.

The blue of the sky grew milky and filled in with an orange hue as the sun settled between two peaks. A long low set of clouds moved up and seemed to cover the bottom edge as the disk sank lower and lower until only one bright beam snaked out across the meadow floor and flashed bright in their faces.

"Oh," she gasped in delight.

The beam wavered for a breath then moved upwards as if trying to grasp the edge of the sky before slipping out of sight. The twilight filled in. One by one the stars began to emerge in the dark velvet of the night sky.

"That is amazing," she remarked.

"Yes, it is. I'm so lucky that I get to see this every night. My father called this his thinking place. He'd come out here each evening and wait for the sun to give its last breath before the night closed in."

"It is just beautiful," she agreed. "Thank you for sharing that with me."

Max reached for her hand and gave it a squeeze. "You and my mother are the only two I've shared this with. Augustus doesn't have time. He's so busy and Melinda…" He gave his head a shake. "She hasn't quite learned the concept of sitting quietly and enjoying the beauty."

"Do you come out here to think?"

Max nodded. "The quiet helps me get my thoughts together. Sometimes, if I'm quiet enough, I can almost hear my father speak."

Callie glanced over and saw the seriousness in his eyes. "I am honored, Max, truly, honored that you would share this with me." She watched as the shadows cast a contour to his face, his strong jaw, the length of his chin all spoke to a good strong character. He made her feel safe.

His head turned back to the scene below.

She let out a deep sigh. A bit of her heart yearned that somehow Max could have been the one to have written to her. Unfortunately, it was Seth.

Callie lifted her face. Her eyes concentrated on the horizon and the developing night. Something brushed her hand. She glanced down at the surface of the rock and found Max's hand beside hers. Her heart skipped a beat. Could she? Should she? She pressed her hand against the hard surface of the stone and her fingers spread out, touching his. There was a hitch in Max's breathing. She didn't move. His hand inched forward. His fingers lay over hers. A thrill of excitement coursed through her. No longer aware of time, Callie sat content with Max's hand on hers.

"Hey, Max!" Augustus voice echoed through the tree line.

The spell, whatever it was, had been broken.

Max suddenly stood up.

Callie jerked her hand away so quickly, that if she hadn't braced her body, surely, she would have toppled over.

"Here. I'm here, Gus." Max moved away toward the edge of the hillside and folded his arms over his chest.

Callie managed to push herself upright as Max's younger brother came busting through the path.

"Ah, there you are," Augustus remarked.

"Yes, I'm right here." Max seemed to be making a point.

The moment turned awkward as Callie caught Augustus glance moving from her to his brother then back again. He lifted a hand and brushed back the lock of hair that fell over his forehead before speaking, "Ah, the guys want to get a team together and play a round of horseshoes."

"Oh, yes, yes." Max put his hands deep in his

pockets. "Sounds great to me." He shifted his gaze to Callie. "Thank you, Callie. I enjoyed the sunset. Are you ready to go back?"

She nodded. Pushing to stand, she moved toward Augustus.

He gave her a strange inquiring look but said nothing, merely held out his arm for her to take. "Allow me to lead you back," he mumbled and sent his brother a daggered glance.

Callie knew this look must have made Max uncomfortable. "Thank you, Augustus," she said and placed her hand on his arm. She shifted her shoulders back and stood tall before she turned to glance at Max. "I enjoyed our conversation, thank you."

"Of course." Max nodded.

Callie noted that his hands were thrust deep into the pocket of his trousers and he refused to look up, almost as if he didn't trust himself.

Head held high, Callie allowed Augustus to lead her back to the barnyard.

THE CLANG of horseshoes rang across the yard. Callie, Melinda, and Bethany sat on the porch and watched as the two teams battled against one another.

The men had placed lanterns around the area to illuminate the two spikes set in the ground and surrounded by loose sand.

"You're up now, Augustus," one of the cowboys called out.

The younger Barringer stepped forward and brought the iron shoe up to line the open end toward the iron post across the way. He took a step back and let the shoe fly. It missed and landed with a dull throb next to the post. Laughter ensued. "Your turn, brother," he called out.

Callie's eyes seemed to naturally focus on Max.

He seemed to stand above the others as he stepped forward. He swung the heavy metal shoe forward. The muscles beneath his shirt strained the fabric as he took aim at the other post.

Unconsciously, she held her breath. This time, a metal clang was heard as the shoe landed on the spike and circled around before coming to a rest on the bottom of the post. Elated, she could not stop the rush of air that burst through her lips. "My, that was a good throw."

"Max is an expert at this game," Bethany replied.

"I don't see why this is just a man's game," Melinda groused.

Callie grinned as she looked down at the young girl sitting on the edge of the porch.

"Don't let it bother you," her mother murmured. "There are things you can do, they cannot."

"Name one," Melinda challenged.

Bethany chuckled. "Men can't quilt and they wouldn't be caught dead doing laundry."

"Those are chores."

"Melinda, what if I asked you to help me do something neither Max nor Augustus would want to do," Callie began. "Would you help me?"

Melinda's head swiveled in her direction. Her face contorted in confusion. "Sure, but I can't imagine what that would be."

"Max showed me the valley to the west of your house, I would love to explore it, but I have a feeling walking would not be the way to go."

"No, it wouldn't. You'd need to ride."

Callie nodded. "That's what I thought."

The tight muscles on Melinda's face relaxed as the idea dawned on her what Callie was about to ask. "You want to learn how to ride?"

"Yes, is it hard?"

"No, it's not hard at all. Not at all. You could learn in just a few days."

Callie rocked slowly back. "I am so glad you think so. I think, if I am going to adapt to this new country, I should learn to ride." She shifted her gaze to the young girl. "So, you will help me?"

"I'd love to." Melinda grinned.

"I think I shall need a very gentle horse."

"I know just the perfect one." Melinda glanced at her mother in order to seek approval. "Princess?"

Her mother nodded. "Definitely a good choice," Bethany agreed. "Princess wouldn't hurt a fly. Melinda learned to ride on her. She's the one I choose if I'm going out for a ride."

"Then Princess it is."Melinda smiled again.

Bethany leaned forward. "Callie, did you bring a riding habit with you?"

Callie shook her head. "It hadn't dawned on me that I would need something to wear riding a horse." She glanced at Melinda. "I don't suppose I could use a pair of trousers like my friend?"

Bethany drew a deep breath. "No, I think that too many people would talk."

"Oh."

They grew silent.

Callie was sure all was lost when Bethany piped

up, "You know, I think I have something that might work. It's a bit dated, but it will do. I'll pull it out and we'll look at it tomorrow."

"I'd like that. But please, let's not tell Max or Augustus. I don't want them laughing at me," Callie admitted. "It will be our secret. Okay, Melinda?"

"If you say so." Melinda gave her a broad innocent smile.

Callie spotted her humor filled look. "Oh, I think I'm in trouble," she whispered.

CHAPTER 9

"*D*o you think I look silly?" Callie asked as she stared at her reflection in the mirror.

Bethany took the straight pins from her mouth to reply. "No, dear, you look just right." With a grunt, Max's mother rose from her kneeling position on the floor. "Now, granted, I was never as wispy as you are. By the time, I came out here, I'd already given birth to two boys."

Callie glanced down at the belt wrapped around her waist. "This will help."

"Yes. I will take another seam along the side tonight. But, the leather belt will do for today." Bethany put her scissors and pin cushion back into her sewing basket. "I don't have any boots, but your high tops will be sufficient. The one thing you will need," her voice trailed off as she turned toward the entrance to her room. "Is a hat." She walked over to the hat tree and plucked up a straw hat. Gently, Bethany held it out to her.

Taking slow steps forward, Callie reached for the large brim hat.

"Can't have your nose getting pink." Bethany grinned.

Lifting the hat, Callie placed it on her head and drew the two leather straps to her throat. "Do I look like a real cowgirl?"

Bethany chuckled. "You do."

Callie couldn't contain her excitement. Reaching out, she grasped Bethany shoulders and gave her a hug.

To her surprise, Bethany returned the affection. "Go, have fun. I know Melinda has been waiting on you."

Her heart light, Callie hurried out the door and down the steps. The split skirt gave her a burst of freedom that she'd never experienced before. Opening the front door, she elongated her steps and moved to open doors of the barn.

Pausing at the opening, she could see a beautiful dark horse tethered between two posts. Melinda stood on the right brushing her hide till it took on a shine

"Hello."

The horse lifted its head and gave a nicker of greeting.

Melinda paused and a smile drew across her face. "You look like you fit right in."

The remark gave Callie the confidence she lacked. "Thanks. Your mom is a wizard when it comes to needle and thread."

Melinda walked forward and slid under the horse's neck to place the brushes in the bucket. "Come say hello to Princess."

Callie moved toward the animal and reached out to touch her nose. The skin below her fingers felt like velvet. The horse pressed her face against her hand and blew out. The warm breath moved across her skin and she relaxed.

"She likes you," Melinda informed her.

"That's a good thing?"

"A very good thing. Horses can size you up with a look and a sniff. You saw that she breathed out but didn't pull her face away. You pose no danger to her. She is comfortable with you."

"That's very good to know." Callie smiled. "I'm

glad you like me, Princess. I hope we can be friends."

"Here."

Callie glanced to Melinda who held out her hand. Curious, she reached out and the young girl dropped a cube of sugar into her palm.

"Hold your hands wide, fingers down so that the cube sits lightly on your flat palm."

Doing as instructed, Callie placed the sweet in the middle of her hand and stretched her fingers down.

"Now, offer it to Princess."

She brought her hand around and before she could blink, the horse stretched its head and she could feel the nimble flurry of the animal's lips against her skin. In the blink of an eye, the treat disappeared. "I see the way to your good graces is a treat."

The animal seemingly understood and shook her head up and down.

"Come on." Melinda laughed. "She'll be looking all day for those. Let's teach you how to saddle a horse."

With Melinda's help and a bit of instruction, Callie soon learned how to put the blanket on and smooth out the wrinkles before placing the saddle on the horse's back. Melinda leaned beneath Princess's belly and brought up the strap. Weaving the leather loop on the girth took a while to grasp. Callie's dogged determination along with Princess' patience paid off and within an hour the bridle was on and she led her out to where Melinda had her pony waiting.

"Always mount from the left," she instructed.

Callie grasped the leather stirrup and lifted her leg high. "Oh my gracious," she gasped and reached for the saddle horn and the back of the saddle.

Feeling her weight, Princess shifted a step to the left making Callie take a bounce step. Her foot lost its hold and she made a clumsy step, nearly falling.

"Try it again," Melinda urged her.

Callie took a deep breath. Her determination grew as she stepped forward and placed her foot in the stirrup. Hands on the front and the back, she visualized herself stepping up.

"Push with your right leg like you're going to climb two stairs at one time," Melinda encouraged.

Callie pushed up.

"Throw your leg over the saddle."

Callie did and hit the seat with a jarring thump.

Princess dropped her rear end and took a quick step forward.

Callie gasped and grabbed the pommel with both hands.

"Whoa, girl," Melinda crooned and ran a hand down the horses nose to steady her.

"Not very graceful," Callie murmured as she adjusted herself into the seat.

"You'll learn," Melinda encouraged. Throwing the leather reins over Princess's head, she walked back to where Callie sat on the saddle. "Now, hold the reins in one hand, like this." She showed her how to place her fingers through the leather by using her middle finger and the other part between her index finger then drew the excess across her palm to lay along her leg. "Princess will neck rein. You pull across her neck to the left and she'll turn that way."

"And if I pull to the right, she'll turn right."

Melinda nodded. "Sit forward, back straight and balance yourself with your legs."

"I remember that." Callie nodded.

"Good. Now wait for me to mount." Melinda strode to her mount and swung easily on board. "You'll be doing that in less than a week," she told her.

Callie raised a brow. "I doubt it, but I'll try and believe you."

Melinda grinned. "We're going to ride up and down the wide trail leading to the ranch today. You're going to learn to sit, walk, halt, turn and trot."

"That sounds like a lot."

"You'll enjoy it."

Melinda was right. Callie did enjoy it. The two of them spent the morning riding back and forth on the mile long trail. With each step, her confidence grew. As the sun rose overheard, she was almost disappointed to hear Melinda call a halt to their lessons. "I wish we didn't have to stop."

Melinda glanced over at her. "I know, but Momma has something for me to do and this is the first time you've been on a horse in years. Riding is fine right now, but you've got muscles that need to relearn how it's done. Trust me, when I say that tomorrow, you'll regret it if we don't stop now."

"Oh…" Callie looked over at the wise young girl. "I hadn't thought about it. I guess, Princess will want to eat some grass and talk to her lady friends."

Melinda giggled. "Now there's an interesting thought, horses discussing people."

They were still laughing when they rode into the barnyard and pulled over to the rail.

"Now, I'm going to hold Princess's bridle and you step off."

"Do it just like getting on, to the left?" Callie inquired.

"That's right." Melinda nodded.

Callie stood up in the stirrups and swung her right leg over the rump of the horse. She paused long enough to move her right hand and grasp the rise of the cantle along the back of the saddle.

Melinda's pony shifted over.

"Am I safe to get down?"

"Sure."

The tone in Melinda's voice had a twinge of amusement. Callie caught it; however the context was lost until she went to find the ground. Her right foot pointed, she pawed in the air. Not feeling anything solid, she shifted and tried to look down between herself and the horse.

"Easy."

Max! Oh, heavens, she didn't want him to see her like this. Her heartbeat ran slammed against her ribs. "I have this," she called out. However, Max nearness to the situation diverted her concentration and Princess must have sensed her growing nervousness. The horse shifted to the right and

Callie could feel herself losing her grip. "Oh!" she cried out as her foot slipped.

"Easy now, I've got you."

She felt his hands span her waist and give support.

Princess calmed.

"Now, let yourself down," Max instructed. "I've got you. One foot on the ground first."

Callie let her right foot down. This time, her toe scraped the ground. She let out the breath she'd been holding and flattened her foot against the earth, before letting her other come out of the stirrup. Her legs trembled. She wasn't sure if it was the horse or the man standing behind her, his hands still on her waist. "Th-thank you," she stammered.

Max said nothing.

She could feel the warmth of his breath against her cheek. Her knees seemed to turn to jelly. Unable to hold herself up, she had no choice but to lean back against Max's strength. "Oh, my," she breathed.

"I've got you," he whispered to her ear.

The sun must have reached its apex for suddenly, Callie seemed to be burning up. The fever caused her mind to wander and her limbs to tremble. "I-I don't know what is wrong with me," she mumbled.

Max's hand ambled slowly down to her hand. "Come over here and sit just for a moment."

She grasped his hand as he sheltered her beneath his other arm. The warmth of his palm at her waist seemed to sear her skin. Callie followed Max's directions and soon she was sitting on a log bench next to the corral. "I don't know what happened," she murmured. She forced her sluggish arms to move and reached up to pull the straw hat from her head. Using it as a fan, she hurried the air across her heated face. "Perhaps, it is the thin air here on the mountainside." She brushed the damp tendrils of hair from her cheeks yet, she refused to look into Max's eyes.

"Could be," Max's voice soothed the race of her heart. "Here."

Forced to look, she could see him hold out a dipper of cool well water. Beside him, Melinda looked on, her eyes wide.

Callie took the dipper and brought it to her lips. The cool water soothed her throat. Taking a deep breath, she glanced at the young girl. "It's not your fault, Melinda. I enjoyed our ride."

Melinda exchanged a look with her eldest brother. "I'll put Princess up."

"No," Callie called out as she turned away. "She's my responsibility. I-I will take care of her."

Max arched one brow at her.

Giving a tilt of her chin, Callie handed Max the dipper. "Thank you. I'm fine."

"If you're sure?"

Callie flashed a smile. "I am."

She rose and stood for a moment. The earth felt firmer beneath her shoes. "Melinda, you must show me the proper way to take care of Princess after our ride."

The girl looked to her brother for permission. Out of the corner of her eye, Callie caught him nod.

"Sure. Come on with me."

Step by step, Callie moved toward the horse.

MAX CROSSED his arms over his chest and watched Callie's faltered steps as she fell behind his kid sister. "Hard headed, Virginian," he murmured. She sure did look pretty sitting up on Princess and riding into the yard though. It had been a sight to see, for sure. Waiting until she'd disappeared into the barn before marching toward it. He would go in and finish putting straw in the stalls. Keep an eye on her, he told himself. The little voice in the back of his mind merely sniggered. Max pressed his lips together and lengthened his strides.

Melinda already had the saddles off the horses when he entered the barn. Callie stood on the left side of Princess running the brush along her coat.

"I'll put the saddles in the tack room," he told her.

Callie's brush stilled.

He added. "You two get those horses brushed down and turned out to pasture."

"Yes, Max," Melinda answered.

He grabbed Callie's saddle first and took it to the small room off the side of the main barn. Lifting it over the wooden saddle tree, he steadied it then turned only to find Callie standing there.

"I would have done that."

He studied her face. A shadow of defiance still lingered in her eyes. Calmly drawing his hands to his hips, Max kept his eyes focused on the ground at his feet. "I know," he murmured. "But I would have done it for Melinda or Augustus because today, I'm in charge of the tack."

Callie blinked. "Oh."

The word illustrated the new understanding of the jobs each person held on the farm.

Her shoulders softened and drooped. "I didn't want you to think I couldn't handle the situation."

Max nodded. "I would have never given that a thought, Callie. You are capable of handling anything."

His words of praise brought a soft pink color to her pale cheeks.

"Go finish your work. I'm sure Princess would love to roll in the grass."

Nodding, Callie turned on her heel and gently walked out of the tack room.

"Hard headed," Max murmured once again, only this time, his lips curled into a soft grin. With saddle and bridle hung in the appropriate places, he shuffled back to the center aisle only to be disappointed to find it empty. "Where did they get to so quick?" he wondered aloud.

Soft laughter echoed from outside. Following the sound, Max found himself drawn to the pasture behind the barn. There, standing alongside the fence, was his sister, Red, and Callie. He moved closer, both curious and a bit frightened of what he might hear. Melinda stood between Callie and Red. With one foot propped up on the bottom rail, she turned so that she could hear what Red was saying. Callie leaned against the fence. She must have been giving him only ear service, for her gaze was fixed on the horses in the field.

Red cleared his throat. "Yeah, them horses is what keeps this ranch financially sound."

"Oh?"

Max delighted in Callie's challenge.

"Yep." Red shifted his stance so that he could see both ladies. "Horse flesh runs this country."

"I thought it was the mines?" Callie queried.

"Gold and silver go bust way too often," Red replied. "If you want to make a living, you need to get into the cattle business. Cattle means horses."

"Oh, my. Well I see," Callie responded. "I hope that Mr. Nolan knows this."

"Old Seth?" Red seemed surprised.

Max felt his stomach plummet to his boots.

"Yes…" Callie turned to him. "You see he's the man that—"

"Callie!" Max yelled.

All three turned to look at him as he hastened his steps to the side of the fence.

"Hey, glad I caught you." He took a quick breath in hopes of calming down.

"What's wrong?" Melinda asked.

"Momma, wants you."

Melinda stared at him, her brow wrinkling beyond her tender years. "Momma?"

Max nodded.

Suddenly, Melinda's eyes grew wide. "Oh...oh yeah." She turned and looked at Callie. "That quilt stuff again. I sort of promised."

Callie drew back from the fence. "Would you like some help? I mean you gave me some lessons on horseback. I can work with you on this quilt."

Melinda seemed to brighten."Sure."

With a nod, Callie put her arm around Melinda's shoulders and they began walking back to the house, but not before Max got a concentrated look from his youngest sibling. Oh, there would be a price to pay for his manipulation. He and Red stood watching them walk back to the house, Melinda's long strides matched by Callie's almost painful ones.

"Funny thing about that conversation," Red drawled.

"What's that?"

"Her talking about ole Seth Nolan."

"Oh? Really?" Max widened his eyes and plastered an innocent expression across his face.

"Yeah..." Red hissed as he folded his arms

across his chest and stared back. "Really, last I heard ole Seth had found himself a bride."

Mouth dry, Max kept his gaze on Callie as she disappeared into the main house. He could feel Red's stare as it bore into his face. Max let out the breath he held and shifted his weight to his left hip. "Has he now," he spoke in a calm even tone.

Red spit on the ground and gave a gruff grunt. "You know it too."

Max rotated his glance to the likable foreman next to him. "I know I promised some good friends to help them out. I'd like this to be our secret, Red. I'd like you to keep that bit of information to yourself for a bit longer, until they get themselves straightened out."

Red shifted his gaze toward the house while Max waited for him to come to a decision. "I been here a long time. I seen your daddy work himself nearly to death to get this house up for your momma. I worked alongside Augustus." he looked back at Max again. "And yourself before any of us realized we were men. I'll keep your secret. I don't need to know why. Only thing is, I hope you don't break that little lady's heart in the process, 'cause I sure thought more of you than that."

Max felt his neck bend as he hung his head. "I

thank you, Red." He extended his hand and they shook. "It's my plan not to break her heart, but to somehow figure a way out of this mess she's been placed."

"Then, you need my wish of good luck."

Max gave a nod as his friend walked back to the barn. "I'm gonna need more than good luck," he murmured. "I'm going to need some help from the good Lord above if this is to be pulled off."

Straightening his spine, Max gave a wary glance at the house and followed Red to finish his chores.

CHAPTER 10

With each day that passed, Callie's confidence grew. By the end of the week, she was the one to rise early and she did so with enthusiasm to throw a saddle on Princess and ride. Once she'd helped Bethany with the dishes, she hurried to change her clothing. Grabbing her straw hat from the dresser, she hurried down the stairway and headed to the front door.

Bethany looked up from her mending as Callie's feet hit the living room floor. "Off again, dear?"

Callie paused. "If you don't mind?"

Bethany shook her head. "Not a bit. I'm afraid the rest of the family has gone to help Augustus move some of the cattle to a new pasture. You don't mind riding alone?"

"No, not really."

Bethany's face eased. "Good. What direction are you headed?"

"I want to explore the meadow to the west."

Bethany put the fabric into her lap. A wistful expression filled her face. "I love that meadow. My husband built a small lookout on the west side of the house."

"Max showed me."

Bethany looked surprised. "He did? My." Her face took on a faraway look. "My husband loved that meadow. He'd sit for hours just looking over it watching the seasons change."

"That sounds lovely," Callie murmured. "Would you like to ride out with me?"

Bethany's smile returned. "Thank you, Callie, but I think not. You go and enjoy but be safe."

Callie made a few steps toward the front door, then turned and walked back to where Max's mother sat. On impulse, she leaned down and gave the older woman kiss on the cheek. "Thank you, for all you have done to make me feel at home."

Bethany reached up and gave her arm a squeeze. "You're like family now, Callie. To be honest, I can't imagine not having you around."

Looking down into her earnest face, Callie could

see a hint of moisture in her eyes. "I'll be back before the afternoon," she promised.

Bethany nodded.

Callie exited the house and walked to the barn.

Princess heard her footsteps and whinnied as she gazed over the fence.

Drawn to the horse, Callie reached inside the pocket of her vest and removed a cube of sugar she took from breakfast. Offering the mare the treat, she rubbed her neck. "Were you waiting for me, girl?"

The horse tossed her head as if to nod yes.

"Shall we go for a ride?" Grabbing the halter, she slipped it over Princess's head and led her from the pasture. In quick succession, she had the saddle and bridle secure. Leading the horse out into the yard, she grasped the stirrup and with acquired grace, she swung aboard. Princess waited for her to get situated. Callie gathered the reins and with a gentle tap of her heels, they hurried across the yard to the trail that led to Rattlesnake ridge.

Once on the road, Callie gave Princess her head and let the horse swing into a soft lope. She found the gait less jarring that the jog. The road was wide enough for wagons and she enjoyed having it to herself. Her hat fell backwards held against her throat by the narrow strips of latigo. A mile or so down the road, she pulled back on the reins and Princess slowed to a stop.

The horse took a deep breath.

She leaned forward and patted her neck. "I know, you want to run some more. However, today we are going exploring in a different direction. Melinda told me the trail to the meadow turns here at the old stump."

She pulled her hand to the right and the reins pulled across the left side of the horse's neck. With a flick of her ears, Princess turned off the main road and onto the narrow trail that snaked its way across the small rise. Callie allowed the horse to pick her own speed and way across the hillside. A grove of tall pines sheltered her from the sun.

"It shouldn't be too much longer."

The horse snorted.

Callie could feel a rise in the trail as she leaned forward and pushed back a low hanging branch. A few feet ahead, the trees thinned and the trail curled downward into the valley.

"Whoa."

Princess came to a halt.

Callie stood in her stirrups and gazed at the scenery below. If she thought the vision of the valley at the bench on the overhang was stunning, nothing prepared her for the supreme beauty that assaulted her senses. Everywhere she looked, right or left, the floor was littered with a perfusion of color. Blossoms of red, white, pink, and blue erupted on all sides, curling in a lush carpet toward the stream that meandered through the center.

"Oh, my," she breathed. "This is a magical place."

Regaining her seat, she tapped Princess's side and the horse moved forward. Even before she made it to the meadow floor, the scent of their blossoms filled the air.

THE DAY WAS GROWING TEDIOUS. The line of cattle stretched out a good three to four miles behind where Max rode. Augustus had taken point with two other wranglers. He'd sent Melinda to the left rear where Red would keep an eye on her and Max could easily get to her should trouble arise. Today, however, the cattle seemed complacent to follow behind the others. The scent of the lush grass ahead acted like the siren's call urging them forward.

A yearling stepped away from the line to snatch a long blade of grass just off the trail. Max gave a sharp whistle. The steer perked up. He ceased his chewing and stared like a kid caught with their hand in the cookie jar. Max gave it a dark glare. The steer's ears flipped and he hurried back to the line.

"Good, just keep it that way," he growled at the bovine.

Max gave his dapple gray a tap with his spurs. The horse moved forward to remind the rest of the herd to keep moving. "I've got my eye on you my inquisitive friend."

The cattle hurried along.

From his right, Max heard the sound of hoof beats pounding toward him. Pulling up, he turned in the saddle to watch his younger brother come abreast of him.

He pulled his chestnut to a halt and dropped his hands to the pommel of the saddle before speaking, "How goes it?" Augustus asked.

"Quiet as usual," Max answered.

"Good." His brother gave a nod. "I'm riding ahead to open the gate. We will have them in and secure before midafternoon."

Max gave a nod. "Good. Since we are close to the Nolan place, I thought I might head over and see Lou."

A somber look took over his brother's expression. "I hope for your sake, Lou and his friends have come up with a plan."

Max looked down at the leather reins in his hands before sending his gaze over to his brother. "I hope for their sake, they have too." Max let go a sigh as he looked toward the horizon. "I can't keep her on the ranch forever. At some point, she's going to get curious and want to go into town. It would be all too easy for someone to tell her the truth."

"And make you look like the king of fools," Augustus added.

Max didn't deny what his brother said was true.

"Course, maybe-just maybe, you should do that."

Max swiveled his head back toward his brother so fast he could hear the muscles snap. A low warning rumble rose from his chest. "What do you mean by that?"

Augustus lifted his shoulders in a shrug. "Well, I was just thinking, if she knew Seth was married, then she'd realize she could either go home or find someone else to get married to."

Max could have sworn his brother struck him. Chest tight, he grappled with the onslaught of anger that rushed through his veins. Even his horse felt it and shifted nervously beneath him. "Go home," he hissed. "That will take some money. You got six hundred dollars lying around the ranch I don't know about?"

"Me?" The surprised expression on Augustus face didn't quite meet his eyes.

For a moment, Max thought he even struggled to keep a smirk from widening his lips. "Just as I thought," Max snapped.

"Well it is true. She could easily find someone else to marry. I mean the ratio of men to women here in Rattlesnake Ridge gives her an advantage."

Max snorted. "Yep, just about any man in town." This kind of talk made him uneasy. Augustus was right. Once word got around, there wouldn't be long before men would be lined up at the door, wanting to court her. It made him itch as if he'd rolled in a mass of chiggers and couldn't shake them loose.

"What about Amos Whitehead?"

"The undertaker!" Max gasped. The shrill tone of his voice seemed to echo across the open valley. "Have you lost your mind?" he demanded. "For one thing, he's in his sixties."

"Lots of folks have May to December romances."

Max clamped his teeth against down so hard they hurt. "No."

"No? What other reason makes Amos no good for her?" his brother demanded.

"For one, she's not suited to be surrounded by death," Max grumbled. In his mind, the image of Callie in mourning clothes made his stomach take a violent roll. The thought of her pale skin continuing in black was like a mark on his soul.

"That's all you got?" Augustus demanded.

Max grew angrier. "Black isn't her color."

For a moment, his brother said nothing. He took a breath and shot a glance his way. Augustus dampened his lips as if he were afraid of his next words. "What is her color, Max?"

Max turned away and gazed across the horizon until he spotted a slump of lupine nestled against an outcropping of rock. "Blue," he whispered. "Blue, the color of lupine in the morning just as the sun comes over the hillside. Or even, lavender like that over there." He pointed to the clump shielded by the shadow of the ponderosa pine.

"I see."

Max caught the laughter in his brother's voice. "You think it's funny."

Augustus drew his hands up, palms facing him and looked back with a wide-eyed innocence that only he could muster. "Funny? Nope, not me." He swung his horse around. "Not me at all, big brother."

Augustus' mount sprang away before Max could challenge him again.

Breathing deep, he watched him ride away but, no peace came to his soul. The thought – the idea of Callie going back to Virginia or finding comfort in the arms of another man made him want to put his fist through a wall. "I need to go see Lou," he grumbled.

Giving the cattle a disgusted glare, Max urged them forward with a shrill whistle. "Get your mangy hides down the trail."

A yearling uttered a mournful bawl as if Max had insulted him grievously. But, their hoof beats grew in intensity as they hurried down the trail coughing up a cloud of dust. Max worked as if someone had a gun to his back. Augustus didn't have to wait long before the last of the cattle streamed through the open gate to the western pasture. And Max didn't wait for the other riders to come to the fence. His lips pressed into a thin line, he threw a dark glaze at his brother.

"I'll be back," he paused. "Later."

"Sure, Max." Augustus kept his head bent over

his tally book. "You go and have a good time. Ride safe."

Max would have loved to give him a parting word to chew on, but there was a part of him afraid his language would have been frowned upon. He pivoted his horse on his back legs and sank his spurs against his sides. The gray leapt forward with such force that clumps of dirt showered those pulling up the corral.

"HEY, WHERE'S MAX GOING?" Melinda cried.

Augustus looked toward his brother's departing figure. His lips twitched. "Going to see a man about a filly."

"Huh?" Melinda's face looked complex. "I don't understand."

Augustus slid his tally book into his breast pocket. "Good."

"Have you gone loco?" she asked.

He leaned over and gave her braid a tug.

"Hey, stop that." Melinda swatted his hand away.

"I hope you'll keep it like that for a long, long while, Mel." He chuckled and climbed down from the top rail. "Come on," he said as he swung into the saddle. "Let's go get some lunch."

RIDING beneath the sign posts of the Nolan Ranch, the only sign of life were a few red hens chasing after bugs and the lazy curl of smoke as it drifted up from the chimney at the rear of the house. Max pulled his mount to a halt in front of the hitching post.

Dismounting, he surveyed the bunkhouse and the barn area. "Like looking a tomb," he murmured.

A sigh escaped his lips as he looped the leather reins around the post and headed up the steps to the porch. His boots echoed at they touched each step. Still, no one came out to confront him. Reaching out, he gave a knock on the door. For a brief moment, there was silence, then the faint sound of footsteps grew closer. Unlike the heavy clump of boots, this sound was more like a whisper as if made by daintier feet.

The knob turned.

Max blinked as a pair of hazel eyes stared back at him.

"Hello."

Her tone seemed to welcome him.

Once the surprise faded, Max reached up and swept his hat from his head. "Morning, ma'am. Is Mr. Nolan home?"

She pushed the door wide and looked back into the house. "Seth, I think someone is looking for you?"

"Coming."

Max twisted his hat in his hands. "I didn't mean to interrupt."

She smiled back. "There's no interruption. Mr. Nolan - I mean my husband, and I were just having a cup of coffee. Please..." She stepped back. "Won't you come in?"

He met her question with a bit of hesitation. "I really just need to ask Seth a question."

"Max, is that you?" Seth's voice called out as he came into view and stepped to his wife's side.

Seeing them together, Max could understand his infatuation. Mrs. Nolan was a few inches taller than Callie. Her brown hair was pulled into a bun at the base of her neck.

Seth placed his arm about her waist and looked as if he were prouder than a peacock. The buttons on his shirt were sure to bust if he didn't get hold of his pride. "Max, it's good to see you." He grinned.

"I'd like you to meet my wife. Ida Nolan, this is our next door neighbor, Maxwell Barringer.

"Ma'am," Max murmured.

"It's a pleasure to meet you." Ida held out her hand.

Timidly, Max took a gentle hold and gave a little shake.

"Please come in, join us."

"I-I don't want to bother you." Max shifted his gaze from Ida to his friend Seth.

The cowboy seemed unable to tear his gaze away from the woman at his side. "It's no bother," Seth replied. "Come on in. You'll be our first guest."

"If you think it's all right," Max said.

Seth pushed the door wider and Max took a step across the threshold.

"Ida, lead the way."

"Of course."

Seth allowed her to take a few steps ahead of them before he gave Max a punch on the arm. "Come on, Max, she won't bite."

Swallowing, Max gave a nod and they moved toward the rear of the house. Passing through the living room, he noted that there were no longer saddles or bits of bridles laying over the tables or the furniture. One thing Ida had done was to tidy up these male quarters. It even had the smell of lemon as opposed to horse liniment.

"Your home looks real nice," Max said as they entered the kitchen.

Seth beamed."My Ida had this place spic and span in two shakes of a cow's tail. Why she's even got Lou and the Allen boys washing up before they come in for a meal. Come on, set a spell. Try Ida's coffee cake."

Max pulled out a chair and hung his hat on the back. "It smells good."

"My mother's recipe," Ida said, as she poured coffee into his cup.

Seth cut a slice of the sweet bread and placed it on a small plate. He picked up a fork and laid it beside the offering before handing it over.

"Thank you." Max could feel all eyes upon him as he picked up the fork and cut a piece of the bread. Placing it into his mouth, he chewed thoughtfully. It was good. Not as good as his mother's, but one thing was for sure, Seth would never go hungry. "Very good, ma'am."

Ida blushed and took the chair next to her new husband.

"So, what brings you all the way out here?" Seth asked.

Max put down the fork. "I was looking for Lou. I had a question for him."

"Lou and the boys are out rounding up some mavericks." Seth gave a chuckle. "Those three are up to something. Said they needed to make some extra money." He leaned forward. "You know, Max, I think the matrimonial bug might have bit them too."

Max tried to dampen his lips but his tongue was too dry. "You don't say," he managed to squeak out. Picking up the mug, he took a sip of the warm coffee. "You make a good cup of coffee too Mrs. Nolan."

She grinned and leaned closer to her husband. "I don't think I shall ever get tired of hearing my new name."

Seth reached out and patted her hands. "I'm thrilled to hear it myself." Seth turned his attention back to Max. "So, what brings you here, is there a problem over at the ranch?"

"No, no." Max shook his head. "I saw the boys in Carson City the other day and they wanted me to hold something for them. I just wanted to know if they were ready for it or not."

"They've not said a thing to me," Seth replied.

He glanced back at his wife. "But I've been a bit busy."

Now, it was Max's time to feel the rise of heat into his cheeks. "I really should go," he said pushing the chair back and rising to his feet.

"Before you go, how about coming out to the barn. I want to show you a new filly, born just yesterday."

"Sure. Sure." Max nodded.

"You won't mind, dear?"

Ida shook her head. "You go. I've had the pleasure of your company for nearly two weeks, I think you need to talk to your friend."

Standing, Seth paused then leaned down and brushed his lips against her cheek.

A pang of want punched Max in his stomach. Lord knows how much he'd give to do the same to Callie's cheek.

"I won't be long," Seth whispered, then turned to Max. "Come on."

They moved through the house and out the front door.

Seth walked beside Max as the crossed the lot to the barn. "It's a grand thing to be married, Max."

Max nodded. "I plan to do that one day."

"You just don't know what you're missing."

Pushing back the barn door, Seth led him over to the back stall where a bay mare stood dozing the sunlight. A tiny filly with the same black stockings lay at her feet. "Isn't she pretty?"

"Yep, she sure is."

"Gonna call her, Ida's prize."

"Nice name," Max agreed.

They grew silent as they watched the foal sleep.

"Tell me something, Seth."

"Sure."

"When did you know Ida was the one?"

Seth grew silent. "First moment I laid eyes on her. Her daddy met me at the station. Ida was sitting in the buggy with the prettiest bonnet on. She turned those green eyes on me and my heart fell to my boots." He leaned on the stall boards. "You know I dated a few of the ladies in town. They were nice, but Ida…" his voice grew soft. "Ida has the voice of an angel. When she speaks, the skies open up and the sun even shines brighter."

Max stood there and listened.

"If she had said no when I asked her, I might have withered up right there on the spot and died. Lord knows, I was nervous. We'd only know each other less than a week. I guess, true love happens like fireworks. It takes just a spark and suddenly everything just burst into view." Seth turned. "Why you asking? Some little filly caught your eye?"

Max almost said yes, instead, he shook his head. "No, I just wondered how it could happen."

Seth's hand came down on his shoulder much as a father's would do. "When it is right, my friend, you will know. You will want to move heaven and earth to make her happy. You can't get enough of looking at her, holding her hand or even pulling her into your arms. It's the best thing that can happen to a man."

Max took a step back and gave a nod. "Thanks, Seth. I'm glad you found your mate."

"You'll find yours. Why I bet she's right in front of your face and you don't even know it."

Max gave a nod.

"You want me to let Lou know you're looking for him?"

"No, just tell him I stopped by." A hand shake later and Max was moving back to his horse.

"Take care, Max," Seth called. "If I can be of any help, just let me know."

CHAPTER 11

*C*allie led Princess to the pasture and opened the gate. "Now, you enjoy your afternoon," she said to the horse, slipping the halter from her head. She stepped back and closed the gate.

Princess looked back, then trotted out to the middle of the field and with Callie looking on, she bent her knees, laid down and rolled in the sweet smelling grass.

"You deserve that." She smiled and made sure the latch was secure in place before walking back to the barn.

Hanging the halter on the hook by Princess's stall, Callie walked to the tack room and slid the buckle away from the saddlebags on her saddle. She reached inside and rescued the armful of colorful wild flowers she'd picked on her journey. Holding the blossoms to her face, she closed her eyes and breathed in the scents. "If I only I could bottle this." She sighed. "And keep it as a memory of my time here on this wonderful ranch."

The flowers cradled in her arms, she moved toward the house.

"Oh, Callie, you're home," Bethany remarked as she closed the front door.

"I brought some flowers." Turning, she was surprised to see Augustus and Melinda sitting at the table. "Oh, I thought you were out working."

Augustus nodded. "We were. Finished early and came home." He leaned back in the chair. "Looks like you had a productive day."

Callie glanced down at the flowers. "Yes, I enjoyed the ride in the broad meadow."

"Those flowers are lovely." Bethany rose. "I'll get you a vase. Just lay them on the table for now."

Callie placed the blooms on the table by the door and walked toward the table. "I need to freshen up a bit before I sit down," she said.

"Use the kitchen sink." Augustus nodded toward the room just off the dining area. "It's a bit closer than running upstairs."

Callie hurried to the kitchen and pulled the wash pan into the sink. Grasping the pump handle, she pushed down three times and the water spit out into the tin pan. Reaching for the bar of homemade soap, she lathered her hands and rinsed.

"Here's one that will do."

Callie turned to Bethany's voice as she moved from the pantry. The clear glass vase had delicate etched designs along the sides. "Oh, how beautiful," she murmured.

Max's mother beamed. "My husband bought that for me. Let's put some water in it." She moved to were Callie stood.

Once again, she grasped the handle and pumped allowing the water to be captured in the glass container.

"It's been a long time since we've had some fresh flowers in the house. Sometimes we forget that spring ends so quickly. Thank you for bringing them back with you."

Together, they walked into the dining room. Bethany placed the vase on the table and with her younger son holding the chair, she took her seat.

Callie moved to her chair and pulled it out.

"I've got that," Augustus spoke softly as he quickly held the back of the chair for her to sit.

"Thank you."

"It's just a small meal today," Bethany remarked, handing the bowl of potato salad to Melinda who, in turn, passed it to Callie.

"Thank you," she remarked taking the bowl and placing a helping on her plate. "I thought Max was with you." Callie placed the bowl on the table.

"Oh, he was," Augustus replied. "He had to go to another ranch to see someone."

"I see." Callie could feel her spirits fall.

"Some sliced chicken?"

"Thanks," she murmured. Sliding one slice onto her plate, Callie felt her appetite ebb away. *So, Max had gone to another ranch to see someone.* Her heart constricted almost to the point she couldn't breathe. *It's not like I have a hold on him. Max probably has a steady young lady he calls on.* Still, the pain settled deep in her chest making her throat feel quite raw.

"Coffee?"

Callie glanced up to find all eyes on her.

"Would you like some coffee," Bethany asked again.

"No, water is fine," she managed to utter.

For a few moments, the only sound was the movement of the utensils across the china plates.

"So," Augustus began, "Which are your favorite flowers?"

"My favorite flowers?"Callie thought for a moment. "I think I like the lupine best. Blue is one of my favorite colors."

"They're so vibrant this year," Bethany agreed.

A bemused smile swept across Augustus face.

Callie felt as if she'd missed the point of the conversation. "Is that important?"

Augustus blinked. "Oh, no, I was just wondering. I think every woman has a favorite flower. Isn't that right, Mother?"

Bethany Barringer seemed as befuddled as Callie. "I suppose," she replied in a quiet tone.

"What's your favorite, Momma?" Melinda spoke up.

"Oh, mine? Hum?" She murmured. "I think I prefer the yellow daisies."

"And you, Melinda?" Augustus inquired. "What's your favorite?"

The young girl grew thoughtful. "I like the Indian paintbrush."

"Very pretty," Bethany replied.

"Yes," Callie remarked, but strangely, she didn't feel any better.

THE LIGHT CAUGHT the design in the glass and the image flickered on the wood of the table that stood behind the couch. Yet for all the glory, the only thing Callie sensed was the illusion of being happy. Unconsciously, she snipped the end of the flower stem and placed it in water. "Why does it bother me that Max went to another ranch?"

She heaved a sigh and reached for another blossom. Her mouth formed a thin line as she clipped the stem on the lupine. "I hope she is pretty." Even as she mumbled the words a cold hand squeezed her heart in response.

Angry at herself, she snatched some Queen Anne's lace to add to the vase.

"Oh, that does look pretty," Bethany murmured walking through the dining room, wiping her hands on the edge of her apron. "I like the mix of colors."

"Thank you." Callie sensed Bethany coming to a stop. She could feel her eyes studying her as she worked. "There," she stepped back and studied the arrangement.

Bethany stepped close and placed an arm around her shoulders. "It's beautiful. Thank you for making my home look special."

The warm words didn't thaw the cold grip on her heart. Max's mother seemed to sense the change.

"Callie, what's wrong?"

She lifted her shoulders in a shrug. "Nothing really." She brushed off her melancholy mood and stepped forward to finger the lacy design of the white flowers. Her emotions rose uncharacteristically filling her eyes with tears. "I haven't heard a word from Seth. I thought—I mean, I hope he has not gotten cold feet."

Bethany's face filled with compassion. She reached out to Callie and placed a tender hand upon her arm. "It is going to be okay. I-I'm sure his work has just gotten in the way."

Even though her chin trembled, Callie nodded. "I think I need to go upstairs for a bit. I-I...." she couldn't finish her sentence.

"Go upstairs. You need a bit of down time."

With a nod, she fled. Nearly running, she rushed up the stairs. Tears blinded her as she held out her hands and reached for the door, swinging it open then pushing it with more force than intended behind her. The sound seemed to echo throughout the house making even the floors vibrate beneath her feet.

Callie leaned against the door. Her hands, palm flat against the wood, she closed her eyes and let the tears slip down her face. For a moment, she gave into the pain that griped her soul. Then, with a sharp swipe of her hand, she brushed the tears away. "I have nothing to cry for," she said aloud in hopes that the words would boost her spirits.

Instead, they rang hollow.

Feeling as if she were losing all hope, Callie hurried to her trunk. Dropping to her knees, her fingers trembled as she fumbled with the locks. Grasping the top, she swung it open. Her eyes searched the contents. "They have to be here!"

She ignored the panic in her own voice. Brushing back the folding stockings and pantaloons, she spotted the bundle of envelopes tied in bright blue ribbon. The frantic beat of her heart slowed. Callie reached for them. Once within her grasp, she pulled them to her chest. With a turn to put the trunk at her back, she melted to the floor. Her arms felt so heavy. Unable to hold them close, she let them fall into her lap.

For what seemed an eternity, she stared at the envelopes and the heavy penned ink that scrawled he name and the p.o. box from back in Richmond. A year ago, they had brought her such unbridled joy.

Yet, today, they seemed faded. The paper crinkled like the dried up dreams she felt. What changed?

Even as the words echoed in the empty chambers of her mind, Callie knew. One word came to her mind, one word that served the purpose of her low spirits.

"Max," she whispered.

The sound of his name filled the room and pressed down upon her shoulders.

"I came here because I promised to marry Seth. I can't go back on my promise."

She sniffled. Her fingers pulled at the ribbon and it fell free across her skirt. Lifting the first envelope, she turned it over and pulled the folded sheet of paper out. The paper was still white and the ceases crisp as she unfolded it.

Dear Callie,

My name is Seth Nolan. I came across your letter at Handley's General Store. I am seeking matrimony and hope I'm not being to bold in taking pen to hand and writing.

Callie took a deep breath.

"No, you were not being bold at all."

She focused on the rest of the letter as he introduced himself.

I am not a rather large man, but stand about average

at five feet, round about ten good inches. I am blonde and blue eyed and turned twenty-nine on my last birthday. I don't have a huge spread, but I run about a thousand head of cattle on my five hundred acre ranch situated near the town of Rattlesnake Ridge."

"Yes, Seth, I wanted you to write to me. I wanted to come out here, to marry you…I just wish you were here."

She put the letter down and stared at the lace curtains dancing in the afternoon breeze. Leaning her head back on the bed post, Callie closed her eyes. "Please, Lord, let my heart show me the man of my dreams."

Behind her lids, an image began to emerge. She held her breath, but instead of the blonde blue eyed man she'd envisioned, a taller more muscular image with dark hair moved forward. Her eyes flew wide. Her right hand rose to try and keep the word from tumbling across her lips. But despite her efforts, his name tumbled forth.

"Max!"

THE HOUR HAD GROWN LATE. Despite the need to head home, the desire evaded Max.

"You need me to freshen that drink, Max," Dobson inquired as he paused to wipe the wide pine bar.

Max tilted the glass of beer toward him and stared down at the liquid. It wouldn't help him to think, but it would sure ease the pain and drown his sorrows. His lips twisted. He gave a shake of his head and answered, "No."

The bartender continued to move his towel over the invisible spot.

Max tilted his head to catch the man's eye. "You got something to say?"

Dobson gave a shrug. "It's not like you to come into the bar and hang out, Max. You didn't even do it when your Pa passed." He lifted his brow and took a breath before finishing his statement, "I just thought you needed a good ear to talk to."

He let the words wash over him. Dobson was right, he needed someone to talk to, but a bartender wasn't the best option. Max took a deep breath and swallowed. "Thanks, maybe next time."

"Anything you say, Max."

He waited for Dobson to move away, then grasping the glass mug, he moved toward the booths along the side. His glass slid along the wooden table as he took a seat. Tilting his hat forward, he hunkered down for the wait. If consistency made the cake, Lou or one of the others would be coming in for a quick drink.

"I need to talk to them," Max mumbled.

The sound of boots and deep laughter drew his attention to the doorway. Sure enough, all three cowboys walked in. His eyes narrowed as he slowly stood. He watched them moved up to the bar and hook their boot heels onto the brass rod at the foot of the bar. His steps were measured as he moved behind them.

"Beer," Lou called. "One for my friends as well."

Dobson poured three mugs and sent them sliding down the length of the pine.

Max waited patiently for the right time to spring his trap.

Lou lifted his glass. "To the ladies."

"To the ladies," Teddy and Dill echoed in unison.

Lifting the glass, Lou's eyes caught Max's reflection in the mirror behind the bar. The mouthful of beer choked him. Sputtering, he sent droplets flying across the bar.

"Easy there, Lou."

"Hey there, watch yourself," Dobson called angrily. "I'm not cleaning this bar all day long."

"Sorry," Lou coughed as he spoke.

Teddy who was standing next to him pounded his back. "You all right, Lou? Ain't like you to choke on your drink."

"Maybe it's his conscience," Max spoke.

Teddy's hand paused midway. He turned his head and his eyes grew round.

Dill's head gave more of a jerk, but he spoke first, "Howdy, Max, didn't think we'd find you having a beer?"

He studied them for a moment. "No, I bet you didn't. Why don't you boys come over to my table? I think we have a matter to discuss."

Lou picked up his mug. "Yeah."

Max raised his arms to show them the way to his booth, with Lou in the lead, then Teddy and his brother followed.

"Good to see you, Max," Lou began as he took his seat across from the foreman of the Nolan ranch.

"You too." He glanced at Teddy and Dill sulking around undecided on where to sit. "Sit over there beside Lou, Teddy. Dill sit by me," Max directed.

The two took their places.

Max wrapped his hands around the glass as the silence grew. "So, I've had Miss McBride around the ranch for nearly a week." His eyes sent daggers at each of the conspirators. "How goes the raising of the money to send her back?"

Lou reached up and pulled at the bandana tied around his throat. "Well, it's like this, Max. We've been working some odd jobs."

"Odd jobs," Max repeated.

Dill nodded. "Yeah, we took a load of wood out to the mine for Cameron. Got some mavericks rounded up and in the south pasture."

"We're plan on herding them over to Reno and sending them down by rail to Frisco. There's a good market for beef."

"How much have you saved?"

Lou glanced at the boys. "We had some expenses."

"Uh huh." Max hissed.

Lou grimaced and leaned to the right to pull a small group of bills from his pocket. "Got fifty-four dollars, if you count our pay for this week."

Max hung his head. "Fifty-four dollars isn't much. At this rate, it will be another six months before there's enough money to send her back." He shook his head despairingly. "We need to come clean. It isn't right to keep her in the dark."

"You can't," Lou hissed. He lowered his voice

and leaned forward. "We could lose our jobs, Max. You don't want to be a part of that, now do you?"

"Should have thought of that before," he growled. "I've got things to do. I can't play nurse-maid another day."

Lou's hand shot across the table and grabbed Max by the arm. "Please."

The urgency in Lou's voice made Max pause.

"Give us just a little more time."

Max drew his arm back. "Look Lou, that woman deserves better than this. She gave up a lot to come out here and marry and you...you messed it up because you brought her out here under false pretenses." His tone grew harsher with each word.

"I'm sorry. I didn't think he'd marry someone else."

"Well...he...did." Max paused at each word.

Lou hung his head.

Max planted his stare at each man until they turned their gazes to look down at their drinks.

"She's a lady. That's what Caledonia McBride is – a lady. And you three aren't fit to scrape the mud off her boots. Out of my way." Max's arm shot out and pushed Dill from the booth. He turned and placed his hands on his hips. Anger made his blood boil. This time, he didn't hold back. "You three have one more week. Then by heaven, I'm going to come clean and tell her myself."

The three cowpokes sunk down against the booth.

"One week." He snarled before spinning on his heels and marching out the saloon doors.

Max let his horse gallop as he beat a path out toward the foothills. The beat of the animal's hooves mimicked the raw throb of his heart. A mile or so from town, his mount slowed. Remorse overcame him and he slowed the animal to a walk.

"I'm sorry, Bandit." He leaned down and brushed his hand across the damp neck of his dapple gray. "I'm taking my anger out on you."

He let the dust of the town and the reluctance of the three cowboys to come clean slip away.

"I wish it was easy to come clean. To tell her, that it was a mistake. Lou and the boys made a foolish mistake trying to help a friend."

The words he spoke aloud even had a hollow ring to his ears.

"I need a better way to come around this," he grumbled.

Bandit snorted and gave a shake of his head.

"Why does telling the truth hurt so much?" Max took a deep breath and let it out slowly from his lips.

The rest of the way back to the homestead, he mulled his options. Pulling into the yard, he stopped in front of the barn and unsaddled his horse. After giving Bandit a rubdown, he turned the horse into the paddock and put his tack back in place.

The sun was dipping low in the sky. Several of the wranglers sat outside enjoying the last rays of the sun. Red gave him a nod as he walked past.

Max didn't quite meet his eyes. His long strides ate up the ground as he crossed to the house. Opening the door, he found his family seated at the table.

One seat was vacant – Callie wasn't there.

CHAPTER 12

*M*ax tossed his hat onto the table and walked to his chair at the table. "Sorry I'm late," he murmured.

He heard the clatter of a fork on the china and glanced over to his brother.

Augustus wiped his mouth with his napkin. "Did you get your business taken care of?"

Max pressed his lips into a thin line. "I met up with who I needed to see." His words were cryptic but he could see by the twitch of his brother's lips that he understood the hidden meaning. "I'll just go in the kitchen and wash up."

"Please do," his mother replied. "I believe you have the scent of Dobson's about you."

Max hung his head. "Yes, ma'am," he mumbled

and cast a glowering look at his brother, who ignored him and picked up his fork.

Stomping to the kitchen, he gave the handle a hard push and the water flew into the tin sink. He grabbed the bar of homemade soap and rustled up a lather. Plunging his hands beneath the water, he scrubbed the dirt from the trail away. Snatching the towel, he wiped the moisture from his skin and hurried back to the table.

"Sorry for being late," he offered the apology as he slid into his seat.

"No apology needed if you were working on a job," his mother replied.

Still, her voice was crisp and Max knew she disapproved.

He slid his napkin into place on his lap and reached for the plate of beef. "Uh, where is Callie?" he finally asked the question that hit him when he first came in.

The table went silent.

Max paused and glanced up.

Melinda looked to her mother and then spoke, "She's up in her room."

Max put a fork of the sliced roast onto his plate. "She sick?"

Melinda picked at the vegetables on her plate.

"No, not sick." Her answer was a hair above a whisper.

Max put his utensil down. "Has anyone asked her?"

Augustus looked down at his food. "I knocked on her door. She said she was not feeling well."

Again, Max could feel his anger rise. Reaching for the napkin, he tossed it onto the table and half rose from his chair. "Does anyone here have any feelings or concern for our guest?"

The fury in his voice made Melinda flinch as if he'd swatted her.

His mother lowered her fork and stared at him as if he had grown another head.

"Apparently, you do," his brother muttered.

Max leveled his resentment in his brother's direction. "What's that supposed to mean?" he snapped.

Augustus shrugged. "Nothing."

Max pushed his chair back with his legs. "I'll be back."

As he moved toward the stairway, he could hear his mother's comment.

"What in the world has gotten into Max?"

What in the world? What in the world? The question leapt through his mind with each step along the stairs. *Callie. Callie has gotten to me.* He paused at the top step and took a deep breath. Lord knows, he was finding himself falling deeper and deeper under her spell. His hand hit the top of the banister. Pain shot through his palm. Max lowered his gaze to the carpet and tried to get a hold of his emotions. "She's in love with another."

But Nolan is married. His conscience reminded.

"But she doesn't know that." He grimaced.

He glanced at the closed door and took a calming breath. His steps were slower, measured, without angst as he moved toward her room. Standing at her door, he paused to listen to see if he could hear any movement.

None.

Max lifted his hand and gave a soft knock. "Callie." He leaned his head against the wood. "Callie, it's me, Max."

The bed springs beyond the door creaked.

He closed his eyes and in his mind, he could see her moving toward him. Those blue eyes large and wondering, just the kind of eyes a man could drown in if he let himself be drawn in.

"I-I'm not feeling well, Max." There was anguish in her voice. He pressed his palms against her door. "Are you ill? Do I need to ride for a doctor?"

"No, no, Max. I'm just very tired."

Something was amiss in her tone. His hand went to the doorknob only to find it locked. "Callie, let me get my mom…."

"No. No, Max. I just need a good night's sleep. I'm tired. I…." she paused. "I will see you in the morning."

He listened to the strain of her voice. Laying his forehead against the wood, he whispered, "Are you really okay?"

When she didn't answer, he called out again, "Callie?"

Silence met his ears.

Max pushed away from the door and with one last glance, headed back down the stairs.

CALLIE LEANED AGAINST THE DOOR, her forehead touching the wood, her palms against the smooth surface. The tightness in her chest seemed to squeeze the emotions from her heart as a tear trickled down her cheek. From beyond the barrier, the sounds of his boots padding against the carpet grew distant with each passing second. Slowly, her hands balled into fist as she resisted the urge to grasp the doorknob and throw open the door to see the one thing that made her feel safe.

All too soon the sounds of silence drifted from the hallway. Turning, she pressed the back against the wood in the hopes of drawing strength. Her right hand brushed away the moisture from her cheeks and she pushed away. Three steps took her to the bed where the letters Seth had written were strewn across.

"I'm here to marry Seth Nolan. I must remember that. When I meet him, all this silliness will be forgotten."

The statement did little to sweep away the sadness that tempted her soul. Leaning, she reached out and gathered the letters she'd spent all afternoon reading.

"I must remember why I am here."

She sat on the edge of the bed and retied the letters with the ribbon. Holding them close to her heart, she stared at the chest she'd brought all the way from Virginia. From where she sat, she could see the embroidered pillowcases, the toweling with the crocheted lace, the beautiful quilt she pieced by hand, all waiting for his call.

"And yet, here I am nearly a week in Rattlesnake Ridge and not a sign of my intended."

Her brow furrowed as the tension built. "Why hasn't he come?" she murmured and clutched the letters tighter. "Has he gotten cold feet?"

Her arms grew heavy and they slid to her lap.

"What am I going to do if he doesn't want to marry me?"

The quiet gave her mind time to mull over the idea.

"I could talk to Mr. Winthrop. Perhaps, there is a clause in the contract about alienation of affection."

The dread of the unknown invaded her heart and the shadow of humiliation threw a blanket about her shoulders.

"I cannot think about this. I need to focus on the positive." She moaned and placed a hand to her throbbing temple.

"I will go to town tomorrow. I will make a purchase at the General Store and check out where Mr. Winthrop's offices are located. Perhaps, there is a posting of jobs that are suitable for a lady. I will not return to Virginia. I will not."

Her last statement took on purpose. Callie rose from the bed and placed the letters back into her trunk. She closed the lid and refastened the buckles. With a sigh, she moved toward the dresser and picked up her hair brush. Sitting down in front of the mirror, she carefully removed each hair pin and shook free the mass of blonde hair. She brought the brush up and pulled it down. The image across from her dissolved into a blurred reflection. Her chin began to wobble. The brush fell to the floor and Callie dropped her head into her folded arm as a sob tore from her throat.

Ten minutes later, somehow, Callie managed to drag herself from the dresser to her bed. Sleep took a long time to come. Her dreams were filled with going to the door after hearing a knock but her hand never seemed to be able to reach the knob. She could hear a voice call out to her, then another. The tortured dreams caused her toss and turn. Finally, beyond exhaustion, she fell into a deep slumber.

The sounds of birds chirping drew her back to the present. Opening her eyes, she pushed back the tangle of hair that lay over her face and drew a deep breath.

"It's not early," she murmured, looking at the shaft of light that pierced the window and drew its long finger across the wall.

She lay still and listened to the sounds out in the barnyard. A few chickens, yet no sounds of the wranglers saddling their mounts to head out.

Pushing back the covers, she rose and padded to the window and looked out.

"Vacant."

She glanced at the corral and made note that Max's horse was not in sight. Stepping back, she pulled her hair to the nape of her neck and glanced around. "I need to get dressed. I should not keep Mrs. Barringer waiting."

With quiet efficiency, she drew her clothing on and fixed her hair into a loose bun on top of her head. Satisfied with her appearance, she opened the door and moved toward the staircase.

The clink of utensils against china signaled someone was still in the dining room. At the landing, she peeked around the corner and saw Melinda and her mother sitting alone. Relief flowed through her; she was not ready to come face to face with Max or his brother.

She plastered a smile on her face. "Good morning."

Bethany glanced up from the head of the table. A soft smile settled on her face. "I'm so glad to see you; I hope you are feeling better?"

"I am," Callie replied as she moved to her place and pulled the chair back. "I must apologize; I was feeling a bit melancholy yesterday." She took her seat and pulled her napkin into her lap.

"It's quite alright," Bethany replied. "Pass the platter to our guest, Melinda."

Max's sister picked up the platter containing bacon and eggs and handed it to her.

"Thank you. I guess Max and Augustus have left for today?"

Bethany gave a nod. "Left hours ago."

Callie's sighed. "I was afraid of that."

Bethany folded her hands above her plate and gave her a curious glance. "Is there something we can do?"

Callie slid some of the food onto her empty plate. Setting it back in the center of the table, she glanced to Bethany. "I want to go into town."

The table grew quiet.

Out of the corner of her eye, Callie noted Melinda's quick glance to her mother. "Did I say something wrong?" she inquired.

Bethany blinked. "No. No, nothing wrong, it's just…."

When she didn't finish, Callie spoke again, "I've been here for almost a whole week." She picked up her glass of water. "I've yet to see anything of Rattlesnake Ridge."

"Oh."

"Yes, I think it's time I did, don't you?"

There was a momentary look of panic on Bethany's face before she hid it behind her smile. "I agree," she paused. "But I've got no one to drive you."

Callie nodded as she figured that out already. "I think I can ride down, but I had hoped to stop by the general store and pick up a few things for my wedding. I'm sure Mr. Nolan will be coming for me soon."

"Oh, um indeed." Bethany picked up her cup.

"I thought I'd pick up some things for a little needlework project."

Bethany brightened. "I've got plenty of scraps."

Callie sliced a warm biscuit and smeared butter onto it. "I know you do. But I want something special."

Bethany's eyes widened. "Oh, I see."

Silence seemed to grow as they concentrated on their meal.

Melinda piped up, "I could take her."

Callie paused. "Oh, could you? I'd love to have you come along."

Again, Bethany's eyes grew wide. "Oh, Melinda,

dear, I don't know. Two young ladies going into town alone?"

Melinda blinked.

Callie watched the exchange with interest. "Why don't you come with us?"

"Me? Oh, I can't," Bethany stammered. "I – I have some linen to change."

Melinda's face filled with confusion. "Momma, you did that last week."

"Oh? Did I, imagine that. I must be getting old and forgetful." She gave a laugh. "It must be the rugs that need beating."

Callie caught Melinda opening her mouth to object, however a sharp glare from her mother snapped her lips shut much like a turtle latching on to a fly.

"It's not safe." Bethany noted, this time with more force.

Callie wiped her fingers on the napkin. "Oh, but you have an excellent sheriff, don't you? I mean, Mr. Nolan wrote to me about what a safe little town it was."

"Oh, it is safe, for the most part," Bethany added. "Sheriff McCullough is wonderful."

Callie smiled. "Well then, I will be perfectly safe."

AFTER CALLIE GOT up to go and change, Bethany turned to her daughter. "Go tell Red what's going on," Bethany hissed to her as she took the stack of plates from Melinda's hands. "Tell him to stall her. Then, you get on your pony and hightail it to Max."

"Yes, Momma." Melinda hurried to the kitchen door and paused. "Momma?"

"Yes, Melinda."

"Momma, why is it a problem for Callie to go to town?"

Bethany took a deep breath. "I don't have time to explain this to you right now. We'll sit down later. Go."

"Yes, ma'am." The young girl turned and hurried out the open door.

"Lord, of all the times for her to decide she needs to understand." Bethany pressed her palms to her temples and closed her eyes composing herself. With a shake of her head, she reached behind her to undo the apron strings. "Maxwell Barringer, you owe me a new bonnet."

She pulled the straps over her head and tossed the plain muslin across the back of a kitchen chair. Turning toward the archway that led into the dining room, she paused to smooth back the unruly tendrils that flowed around her face. Straightening her shoulders, she moved through to the dining room.

Overhead, she heard the sound of shoes on the floorboards and a door being closed. Her gaze followed the steps to the stairway. Bethany moved to intercept Callie. She positioned herself at the table behind the sofa and as Callie's footsteps moved down the stairs, reaching out to straighten some books. The creak of the stairs grew loud. She shifted her gaze and saw Callie poised at the last stair. "Oh, you got ready so quickly."

Callie stepped down to the floor and adjusted the reticule that hung from her wrist. "It didn't take long." She looked over and smiled. "Are you sure you won't come?"

"Oh, yes, I've much, too much to do. But thank you."

Callie gave a nod.

"Oh, the wind is picking up," Bethany added.

"I saw. That's why I brought my cape," Callie referred to the cloth draped over her arm.

"I'm glad, you know, it is summer, but that wind can be cool."

"Yes."

She watched the young woman moved toward the front door.

Callie picked up her hat from the table and carefully placed it upon her head.

"Let me help you with that cape." Bethany hurried over and took it from Callie. She placed it over her shoulders and smoothed the dark fabric down. "There we go."

"Thank you." Callie nodded as she looped the thick braid over the frog at her throat.

"I'll walk out with you." She held the front door open and allowed Callie to exit first.

"It's a lovely day for a buggy ride."

"Yes, it is," Bethany agreed as they walked into the yard.

Neither spoke as they moved across the barnyard. Stepping into the shadow of the open barn door, both women heard the roar of a male voice.

"Dagnabbit!" Red's hammer flipped from his hand and fell to the dirt.

"Red, what's going on?" Bethany strode forward, her hands on her hips.

"This thing," Red grumbled as he bent over to pick up the hammer. "I'm sorry, Mrs. Barringer, I know you asked me to get this wagon wheel done sooner, but we've had so much going on. Now that

I've got it off, it looks as if the metal rim just wore clean out."

"Is that the buggy I wanted to use?" Callie asked staring at the three wheeled black one seat carriage.

"Yeah, it's the easiest one for lady's to use," Red said with a nod. "Sorry about this, Miss."

"Oh, no." Bethany shook her head. "Callie had her heart set on going into town today."

The wrangler scratched his chin. "Might not be able to."

Bethany noted Callie pressed her lips into a thin line. Thinking quickly, she hoped to divert her next question. "Will we need to get the rim to the blacksmith or can you fire up the forge and do it here on the ranch?"

"If we take it to the blacksmith, it will be at least two weeks before I can get down to Rattlesnake Ridge. Augustus has us heading out to look for strays starting next week. I can fire up the forge but it will take all day to heat and hammer it out."

"Is there another wagon I could use?" Callie inquired.

"Nothing but that big ole buckboard over there." Red jerked his thumb at a large wagon. "But if you ask my opinion, that's way too much for a delicate woman, like yourself, to use."

"I see." Callie crossed her arms and gave the wheel a withering glance.

For a moment, Bethany thought she'd won.

"What about that small surrey there?" Callie pointed to the two seated vehicle with the fringe around the canopy.

The cowboy blinked. "That there is only used for Sunday or special occasions, Miss. If it was to go out today, I'd have to spend most of the night cleaning it up for another run to town."

Callie stood her ground. "I'd think this is a special occasion, Mr. Red."

The use of mister before his name put the cowboy on guard.

"It looks like I would only need one horse. I think I can safely drive that, Mr. Red, if you will hitch it up for me." Callie walked over to where the lead lines hung and picked up a rope. "Please?"

Red glared at Bethany.

She'd lost, her only hope was that Melinda could get to Max and let him know what was going on. Squaring her shoulders, Bethany Barringer gave a nod. "Red, get Poppy from the corral."

"Yes, ma'am."

Callie took a seat on a bale of hay as she

watched Red brush the red chestnut named Poppy. "Do you have to brush her so much?"

Red glanced over the horse's withers. "Yes, ma'am, if you put the harness on a horse that hasn't been groomed, they might get a blister where the leather rubs." His brow furrowed. "They did teach you that in Virginia, didn't they?"

Callie pressed her lips together. "Yes. Sorry."

A sound of hoof beats coming into the yard caused her to turn her head. She recognized the bay horse and rider pulling to a halt in front of her.

"Whoa." Max swung down from his horse and flipped the reins around the hitching post.

Her heart gave a leap. She balled her hands together and pressed them against her skirts. Unable to take her eyes of his slow saunter, she made a mental note of everything he wore from the deep red bibbed shirt, which he kept three of bib's buttons undone just enough so the fabric flapped against his chest with each step. The chink of his spurs on his boots echoed with each pump of her heart. The dark leather chaps that protected his legs seemed like another layer of skin.

"Red, Melinda said you were having a little trouble?"

Red took a deep breath and paused. "Wagon rim

wore clean through. But now that you're here, maybe you can take it to the blacksmith?"

"I could." He paused and turned his attention to Callie. "Morning." Max nodded.

"Morning," she began. "I didn't expect to see you back so quickly."

"Well, it's not a good thing to get told to come back. What are you doing out here?"

Callie glanced at Poppy. "I was hoping to go to town, but it appears to be a losing battle."

Red ignored the conversation and began brushing the horse again.

"Going into town?" The lines around his mouth deepened. "We're going into town tomorrow for church."

"But the stores won't be open." She pointed out. "I wanted to do a little bit of shopping."

"Oh." Max glanced at the surrey. "Don't go to town."

Callie blinked. "Don't?"

Max nodded. He glanced around and then gave a nod of his head toward the outside. "Walk with me, Callie."

She glanced toward the sunlight and hesitated.

"Please."

She wanted to tell him no, to stand up and

demand to go into town. Instead, she gave in. "Very well." She stood up and with Max's gentle hand upon her elbow, they walked into the yard.

He led her over to the corral.

Callie placed her arms over the top rail and stared at the horses grazing on the deep green grass.

"Don't go to town, Callie," Max whispered.

"Why?" She looked over at him. "Why not go to town? What's in town that has everyone so upset that I want to go?"

Max shifted his gaze to the pasture. "I-I don't want you to go."

Callie blinked. "I don't understand, Max."

Something in his face seemed raw and honest as he turned his head and stared straight into her eyes. "I don't want to share you with the town."

"You don't…." Her words faded away.

His expression softened. "Change your clothes and come take a ride with me."

Callie knew she should say no. She should walk away, grab a horse, and ride into town on her own. Yet, there was that unexplainable vulnerability in his eyes that made it impossible for her to refuse. "All right, Max. I'll come with you.

CHAPTER 13

I must have lost all reason. The words echoed across Max's mind as he led Callie through the timberline to a spot he knew by heart. The rounded a small rise and he brought his gelding to a halt. He placed a hand on the cantle of the saddle and looked back. "It's just through here. Watch your head."

Callie gave a nod.

Max bent low over his horse's neck as the bay slipped quietly through the boughs of the pine and into a hidden meadow. He waited for Callie.

Princess's head popped first, then he caught sight of her blonde head nearly laying flat over the horse. Her hat got pushed back by the green branches of the pine. A brush of excitement added the pink to her cheeks and a shine to her eyes.

He waited for her to ride up next to him.

"What is this place?"

"My homestead," Max murmured. His gaze moved around the sheltered cove. "I've started my cabin." He pointed to the foundation of stone and the basic framing of the walls. "Want to see?"

She nodded.

They rode over to the cabin. Max dismounted and held Princess' head as Callie stepped down from the saddle. Taking the reins from her hand, he looped them over the hitching rail that stood before the unfinished work.

"Come on." He held out his hand.

She stared at his outstretched hand.

Max waited half anticipating her to brush it away; half hoping with all his heart she'd place her hand in his.

She dampened her lips and swallowed.

He watched, mesmerized, as her slender fingers brushed his palm. Before she could regret the action, he closed his hand around hers.

Their gazes met.

He offered her a warm smile which she returned.

In that moment, something passed between them. He caught a glimpse of tenderness in her eyes which caused his heart to turn over. *Yes, yes I could love this woman.* The knowledge made his heart skip a beat. It was the same intense feeling he had as a child coming down for Christmas morning. Max led her up the steps and on to the porch.

"This is where I will come to watch the sun in the morning."

"A perfect place for a chair," she replied and stepped closer to his side.

"Two chairs," he murmured.

She glanced up at him, her gaze so tender it seemed almost as a caress.

"Yes," she whispered. "Two."

"Come inside." He led her through the opening for the front door and into the center of the house. "A beautiful fireplace, but you haven't put the mantel on yet."

Callie moved to the rough hewn rocks and brushed her hand across them.

"I picked those up all along the creek bed below the hill. I want to find the right piece of wood to make the mantel."

"Strong wood." She took a breath. "Like you."

Her head turned and once again her gaze seemed full of expectation.

"Perhaps," he breathed the word.

She turned toward the rear of the house. "And over here?"

Max shook his head. He needed to get a hold of his emotions. "Oh, that's where my kitchen will be."

"And will it be big?"

"Yes. Big enough to hold the dreams of a lifetime."

"Then it will be huge, indeed."

Every time his gaze met hers, he could feel his heart turn in response. Somehow, in just a few days, Callie had managed to open his heart to the prospect of tomorrow.

"Why haven't you finished this?"

He lifted his shoulders. "It hasn't seemed right…." He waited for the beat of his heart, then added. "Until now." He looked up at her.

She seemed to be fighting some feeling. A look of pain danced across her face.

It was Seth. Seth and that commitment she had made. He knew it was false, but would she believe him if he told her? The idea that she would be devastated cut him to the quick. The urge to grab her and crush her to his body for protection proved so strong, Max thrust his hands into the pockets of his trousers. "Mom packed us a few things. Wait right here."

"Of course," she nodded.

Max walked away and hurried back to his horse, all the while muttering beneath his breath, "I'm in love with a woman who is in love with another man." He moved to his saddle bags. "That man is married and doesn't even know she exists." He stole a glance back at the cabin and found her walking around looking at the unfinished structure. He lifted the strap and undid the buckle, then paused. In his mind's eye, he could see her, standing there in the middle of the cabin. A warm fire would be flickering sending shafts of light to bathe that golden hair. She'd turn those blue eyes, all warm and inviting to him, and her gaze would be only for him. His gut tightened. They would embrace. Her head would turn up to him and he could claim those strawberry tinged lips.

His gelding shifted. Max didn't feel the hoof until the pressure became too much to bear. "Ow!" he cried out and shoved the horse, who took a step sideways.

"Max!" Callie moved to where the front window would be.

Deep concern marred her features. "Max, are you okay?"

He pulled the meal from his bag. *Dang it, she cared. How can I get her to see me and not Seth?* "Yep," he snapped. "Horse stepped on my foot." He held the food close and shifted his stance to give his foot a shake. Walking past his horse's head, he gave the animal a snake eyed look.

The horse jerked its head up and stared back with a look of wonder.

"Watch yourself, Champion."

The horse snorted and gave a toss of his head.

Callie met him at the steps. "Are you sure, you are all right?"

He moved up the steps masking the slight limp on that sore foot. "Fine, he just stepped wrong and I didn't move my foot."

Her soft smile meant only for him, erased the pain. "Let me help you." She reached for the red and white cloth.

Max let go.

"Let's put it over here, in the center of the house."

Her smile made him forget the misgivings. He moved to help her spread the cloth out on the wide plank floor. She knelt on the edge and he watched her untie the twine that held the food in the brown paper.

"Come on." She patted the cloth.

Max lowered his frame onto the cloth.

"Oh, some of your mother's fried chicken." She held up two yellow wedges. "And this is good sharp cheese. Does this come from the general store?"

"Yeah, the store," Max whispered, but his eyes saw only her not the cheese or the chicken.

She brightened. "Oh, I know what this meal needs."

Before he could react, she was up on her feet and scurrying out to the meadow. Max watched as she gathered a handful of wild flowers that were scattered along the edge of the meadow.

Her cheeks were flushed as she hurried back. "We don't have anything to put them in," she bemoaned. "But I know what we can do." He watched as she placed the fragrant blossoms against the cloth between them. She glanced up. Her smile lighted up her face. His sense shifted up a notch. "But, it still looks beautiful."

"Yes, beautiful."

Max knew he wasn't talking about the flowers. No, he was talking about the woman who had stolen his heart.

Callie stilled. Her expression grew somber.

"Max, why are you looking at me like that?"

"Because, you're a fine-looking woman, Callie." The words came out before he could stop them.

"Max," she began.

"Callie, listen to me, what if..." He took a breath and summoned up his courage. "What if there was a way to stop this?"

"This?" she questioned with a turn of her head. "This what?"

"Marriage, Callie. What if you didn't marry Seth?"

"Max, you're not being reasonable." She sat back and stared at him.

"Am I?" He reached for her hand, but she was too far away. "Callie...."

She pushed away from the floor. "We're friends, Max."

He rose and followed her to the front of the cabin. She stood with her back to him and he placed his hands on her shoulders."I care for you, Callie. I don't know how or why it happened, but I care for you."

"Max, please." She turned her head.

He found her cheek next to his. The warmth of

her skin felt right. The need to hold her close made his knees grow weak.

"I am promised to another," she said softly.

"It can change. We can go and talk to Seth…."

Her fingers found his lips and pressed the rest of the words back. "No. Max. I spent a year writing and I've made promises. What kind of a woman would I be if I failed to keep my promise? I am honor bound." She looked up at him and the pain in her eyes was obvious. "Please, we must stop. Tomorrow, I shall go to church. Seth wrote to me of a boarding house. I will make arrangements to move there until Seth comes for me." Tears made the blue of her eyes glisten.

Her voice was barely above a whisper but her pain cut him like a knife.

"Thank you, Max for all you have done. If this were another day – another time, things might have been different." She moved away.

A deep cold stillness seeped into his soul.

Pausing at the opening, she spoke again, "We must leave it at that."

He watched her pause at the framing. Her head bowed. Her shoulders slumped. She didn't look back. "We must remain friends." Her voice lowered to a soft melancholy refrain. "No matter what we are feeling."

Max didn't need to watch her leave. He knew he has pressed too far and made a mess of things. He closed his eyes as he heard the creak of leather as she mounted and the sound of the horse moving away.

Max let the silence of the mountain settle over him. The breeze along the hillside picked up. The tall pines began to sway and give way to that long lonesome wail that filled the valley and echoed the pain in his soul.

THE SHADOWS HAD LENGTHENED by the time Max returned. Lamps shown in the windows and the barn door had been left ajar for him to enter. Dismounting, he led his horse inside and over to his stall. Inside, he flipped the stirrup over the saddle horn and began to loosen the girth.

"How's it going?" a familiar voice asked.

Max paused and glanced over as his brother stepped from the shadows. "It's going." Max turned his attention back to the girth strap. Out of the corner of his eye, he watched Augustus move toward the stall and rest his shoulder against the four by four that made one edge of the structure. "Callie came back early."

Max ignored the comment.

"She went straight to her room after saying she was too tired to eat."

Max grasped the pommel and the back skirt of the saddle and pulled it from his mount. Slinging it over the rails, he let it rest before looking over at his brother. "Maybe she was."

Augustus raised one brow.

Max turned away.

Yeah, he didn't believe those words either. He took the bridle off the horse and hung it over the pommel of the saddle so it wouldn't get lost.

"You want to talk about it?"

Disgusted with the hand dealt him, Max picked up a brush and began to groom the horse. "Not particularly." He brought the brush down across the horse's back smoothing his coat with his hands as he went.

"Did you tell her the truth?"

Max paused. "No."

"Brother, I have nothing to do with your business, but you can't keep this lie going. It's eating you inside. I can see it. Shoot, anyone can see it that looks at you. You're in love with Callie. If you want to keep her, you are going to have to spill the beans."

"Who says I love her?" Max words came out like a low growl rumbling from his chest.

To his surprise, his brother chuckled.

"That."

"That what?" Max inquired.

"That," Augustus replied. "That growling and hem-hawing."

Max grunted in an attempt to hide behind his pride. "I don't know what you are talking about."

Augustus howled. His laughter filled the barn and reverberated like a clap of thunder. "My dear brother, you have it bad." When he collected himself and wiped the moisture from his eyes, he added. "Why don't you just tell her the truth and ask the woman to marry you?"

Max hung his head. Leave it to Augustus to come to the crux of the matter. The scab peeled from the wound, he glanced up. The look on his face sobered his brother. "I tried, Gus. She is still in love with the Seth she met in those letters."

Augustus looked stunned. Then his head began to move side to side in slow motion. "Did you tell her about Lou, Dill, and Teddy?"

Max shook his head. "Didn't give me chance, before she wanted us to just be friends." He crossed under the horse's neck and gave the gelding a pat on the side as he left the stall.

Together, the two men stood and watched the horse swish its tail and settle down for the night.

"I'm going to head out tomorrow. She's going into town to the boarding house. I want you to take her Augustus. Get her settled." Max could feel the despair falling around his shoulders. "You tell Miz May that Callie's money is no good. Once this has all blown over and Callie's gone, I'll settle up."

Saying the words, *Callie's gone* caused Max's heart to ache. He turned only to find his brother's hand on his arm.

"I don't like this, Max. Callie won't be there three hours before the story will get out."

"I know," Max's words were sullen.

Augustus squeezed his arm. "Then stay," he urged. "She'll need a shoulder to lean on. Let it be yours."

"I've hurt her, Gus. I've hurt her bad. And once she finds out, I don't think she'll trust me any farther than she can throw me."

"You're not giving her credit, brother. Once

Callie finds out what happened, she's going to see it as a way to release her from her promise."

Max looked into his brother's face. "You didn't see her face, Gus." He shook his arm free and with wooden steps moved toward the barn entrance.

"I still say you're making a mistake," Augustus raised his voice so his brother could hear.

Max paused, then without responding, walked away.

He let himself and quietly closed the door.

The heavy click of the lock drew his mother's voice from the kitchen. "Max?"

He put his hat on the rack hanging by the doorway and crossed to the kitchen. "Yes ma'am."

His mother turned and dried her hands on the edge of her apron. "Max, I was so worried."

He hung his head. "I didn't mean to upset you."

"Come, sit." His mother wiped off the small table and patted the top in front of the chair.

Without a word, he followed her directions and took a seat. The silence was as long and as uncomfortable as it had been with Callie.

She slid a cup of coffee before him. "Drink this."

Max lifted the warm cup to his lips and took a sip.

"You look miserable. Tell me, is it true? Callie said she is leaving."

He put the cup down and gave a nod.

"Max, did you tell her?"

"Tell her what? The truth." He groaned. "She's in love with another man, Mother."

"Oh, Max," his mother's whispered voice consoled him.

He took a deep breath and felt his throat grow raw. "I tried," he groaned. "But I didn't have the right words."

"Oh, sweetheart." Her hand found his shoulder.

"I'm so sorry, Mother. I failed you and Callie." Max pushed away from the table and moved toward the doorway. "My words weren't good enough."

CHAPTER 14

*C*allie stared at her reflection in the mirror. There were dark circles beneath her eyes. Sleep had been nothing but an elusive specter. Giving up before the sun even rose, she'd carefully packed all of her things in the trunk at the foot of the bed. Dressed in a dark skirt and white blouse, she sat on the edge of her bed and waited for the family below to finish their meal. Melinda had come by and asked her to dine, but she couldn't. She didn't have the heart to sit beside Max knowing that….

"Knowing what?" she whispered.

Her heart answered. *That you have fallen in love with him.*

She closed her eyes; resigned to the truth.

"What am I going to do?"

Glancing to her left, she spied the small, white leather bible which survived the journey from Richmond. Picking it up, she opened the text and scanned the verses.

She read the words from First Corinthians, "Love is patient, love is kind. It does not envy, it does not boast, it is not proud." She took a deep breath. "It does not dishonor others…."

She could not read more.

Closing her eyes tight, Callie prayed, "Please, Lord, please help me to know what to do. I came out here to this new land to offer myself in marriage to a man who has written the kindest letters and now…" She hiccuped as the tears threatened again. "Now, I find myself drawn to another. I dishonor Seth with my wanton ways. Help me restore my honor in Your eyes. I am so confused…" Her words died away as footsteps came to the door.

A knock echoed.

"Yes," she murmured brushing away the moisture from her cheeks.

"It's me, Augustus."

Callie said nothing.

"We're about ready to go into church."

"Yes." Callie rose and placed the small bible into

her reticule. Walking to the door, she paused at the trunk to pick up her bonnet before she opened the door.

Augustus stood waiting.

She glanced back at the trunk. "My things," she began.

"I'll pick them up after church."

She nodded.

He backed away as she stepped into the hallway.

"Callie," he began. "I wish you'd rethink this. Things aren't what they seem."

"Thank you, Augustus. But I can't. I must do what is right. If only Max and I had met under different circumstances."

He nodded. Taking her by the arm, he led her down the stairs.

Callie was pleasantly surprised that the main room of the house was empty. They crossed the floor and he led her out onto the porch. From the shadows beneath the porch covering, she could see Red and two other wranglers mounted behind the surrey. Bethany sat in the front seat beside Max.

As they walked toward the rig, Callie could only note how handsome he appeared in his dark suit.

He glanced at her only as she came to a stop at the rear of the surrey. "Morning, Callie."

The sound of his voice was warm and comforting to her ears. If only they had met on other circumstances. "Morning, Max." She placed her reticule on the seat and with his brother's help stepped into the surrey. Straightening her skirts, she waited as Augustus mounted.

"Head up," Max called and gave a snap of the reins against the chestnut's rump and the horse leaned into the collar to pull the buggy forward.

"I bet you're excited to see Rattlesnake Ridge," Melinda leaned over and whispered.

Callie didn't say a word, she merely gave a nod.

The wind was blowing from the southwest and it caught the scent of soap from Max's skin. She breathed deep hoping to keep that as a lasting memory. Winding down the trail from the ranch, they crossed over the stream that fed the big meadow. The trail fed into a wider path.

"This is used by the wagons going up to the lumber operations," Melinda explained. She pointed to the gap between the rise of the hills. "We'll go through that and then down to the valley where the town sits."

As the wagon wound down to the outskirts of town, she could see a flurry of activity. Folks walking along the boardwalks, others riding their horses, still more were in buggies or wagons, yet all were headed in a singular direction. Above the buildings on Main Street, she spotted the tall steeple of the white church.

Bethany turned to speak to her, "Our town seems to be having another one of its growing spurts." She pointed to the building on the right. "That's the records office and this house coming up on the left, across from the bank is the boarding house run by Miz May."

Callie swallowed as they moved closer. It was a nice building, but it wasn't as homey as the Barringer ranch. A sudden pang of homesickness swept through her. It would be hard to leave the place she'd grown to love. "Can I open an account at the bank?"

Bethany paused. "You can, but keep a good account of your sums. Sometimes they are a little off."

Her comment made Max give a gruff laugh.

They turned onto another wide street.

"What's that building on the corner?" Callie pointed to the right.

"That's the saloon."

Callie could feel the heat rise in her cheeks. "Oh."

Max guided the surrey to the front of the church. The ladies waited while Augustus and the others dismounted. Bethany was the first to depart, escorted toward the church by Augustus. Red helped Melinda down and offered her his arm.

Callie scooted to the edge of the surrey and looked up expecting to see the second drover. Instead, Max waited patiently.

For a moment, they stared into each other's eyes. A multitude of regret surfaced. She wondered if he knew just how hurt this all made her feel.

"Callie."

Her name rolled off his lips making her heart ache. Be brave, she told herself and held out a tentative hand.

Max reached for it and the warmth of his touch swirled up her arm, creating a desperate need for his closeness. She leaned out and pressed the toe of her shoe against the metal brace. His hand moved to her waist forcing her to place both against his shoulders as Max lifted her down. For a brief moment, she held on longer than necessary, her strength gathered, she pushed away.

"Callie," he murmured.

The sorrow filled tone of his voice made her ache once more for his touch.

With a shake of his head, he offered her his arm.

She placed her palm upon the sleeve of his jacket and they walked toward the group gathered by the steps.

"Callie, I'd like for you to meet our church leader, Reverend Alistair Brown," Bethany said as she pulled Callie to stand beside her. "Reverend Brown, this is our guest, Caledonia McBride. She's traveled all the way from Richmond to be with us."

"Ah, well aren't you a bonny lass." He smiled and shook her hand. "Welcome to Rattlesnake Ridge. I hope you'll be staying."

"For a while," Callie replied.

"My wife, Adeline."

Callie turned toward the formidable woman standing beside him.

Her grey hair pulled back in a bun at the nape of her neck gave her an austere appearance, however the green eyes that stared back at her carried a hint of laughter. "We are pleased to have you here today, my dear. I hope you enjoy the service."

"I'm sure I will." Callie suddenly regained her composure. "I'd love to talk to you in the coming days," she murmured.

"Oh?" Adeline's brows arched.

Callie leaned forward. "It is about matters of the heart."

Adeline glanced back to Max. A bemused expression pulled the edges of her lips upward. "Oh, I can imagine what it might be about. Will you be in town?"

She glanced at Max before looking back to Mrs. Brown. "Yes, I plan on taking a room at Miz May's."

Her answer earned her a scowl from the tall man just behind her.

The toll of the bells began and the congregation, including the Barringer's moved inside the church.

Callie found herself wedged in between Mrs. Barringer and Melinda as they moved down the center aisle.

Midway of the chapel, Mrs. Barringer stopped and pulled her daughter in front of her. "Go down to the end," she instructed.

Melinda glanced at her mother, then slid into the pew. Mrs. Barringer followed.

Callie moved in and as they sat down, she realized Max was seated next to her, followed by his brother. The other wranglers moved behind them. For a small church, there was a good turnout, nearly every seat was taken. Callie watched as Mrs. Brown moved forward and took her seat in the first row.

"Here," Bethany pressed a hymnal into her hand.

Callie took it only to find Max balancing the other side. His nearness unnerved her. She tried to concentrate but found her mind drifting back to the man beside her. So lost in thought, she nearly missed the cue to stand. Once again, Max's steady hand came to the rescue.

I must look at something else.

She gazed between the heads and shoulders and watched the young woman skillfully move her hands across the keys of the upright piano. A group of six men and women stood to the right and began the hymn. Max's voice was beautiful, bringing tears to her eyes. When the song was finished, they sat down and Callie had to wipe the moisture from her lashes. Someone pressed a white linen handkerchief into her palm. She glanced to her right.

Max gave her a soft smile.

Look at the colored glass.

Callie concentrated on the way the light fractured as it came through the colored glass behind the pew.

Reverend Brown moved through the calls for prayers for the sick, the need for help on ranches and just as he was about to open his sermon a ripple of whispered rocked the congregation. Every head turned, including her own, as a tall man wearing a blue suit, walked in with a beautiful woman on his arm. He spoke to a man three pews behind them. The man scooted down and he allowed the woman to take her seat with his being on the end.

Callie heard Bethany Barringer utter a small gasp.

Max tensed.

"I'm so glad we can all be here together," Reverend Brown began, drawing the attention back to the front of the church. "I want to bring your attention this week to the words of inspiration found in the book of Ruth. Famine struck the land and many died. One such was the husband of Naomi and her daughters-in-law, Ruth and Orpah."

Callie felt her heart go still. She'd heard this story many a time in Virginia.

Reverend Brown continued to tell the story, the words that Naomi spoke echoed, "It is better that you return home where you can find husbands and fulfill your destiny. But, as we know, Ruth insisted on staying. It was her courage and loyalty to both God and Naomi that opened up the path for her to find a loving husband in Boaz."

Callie tried to swallow. The words he spoke seemed to be leveled right at her.

"We've had many come from all over this great land to become wives and mothers, for filling their dreams and helping to breathe into this town the gift of life." Reverend Brown walked around the pulpit, his smile growing. "And ladies, we thank ye, for there is nothing worse than a town which is not grounded in the common decency of a loving hand. Men, look at those who have chosen to give their life to you and remember those vows to love honor and to cherish. Strength in family will settle this land."

He moved back behind the pulpit.

Yes, I came here to marry. I must be loyal. I must remember why I am here.

Callie felt her feet find firm ground.

"I want to take a moment and recognize our newest citizen." Reverend Brown smiled. "Most of you know, Seth Nolan."

Callie's head jerked. *How did he know?*

"A fine young man, a few weeks ago he went away on ranch business."

Yes, yes, just what Max told me. Callie's heart began a rapid hammer against her ribs.

"Well, it has come to my attention, that he has

found his heart's desire."

Callie's hand was on the back of the pew in front of her.

"Dear friends, please welcome the newest member of our community…."

She scooted to the edge of the bench.

"Callie, no," Max hissed.

She stood.

"Mrs. Ida Nolan."

Callie gasped.

She turned as all eyes gazed up her, then the woman standing three rows back. Bewildered, she watched as the tall man in the blue suit rose and lifted the woman's hand to his lips.

"We congratulate you, Seth."

Her legs gave way. Callie collapsed onto the wooden seat.

"Callie. Callie, I'm sorry," Max whispered.

Stunned, she turned to stare at him. "You knew. This is why you kept me on the ranch. You knew!"

Max tilted his head as if to shake no, then paused. "It's not what you think?"

She swallowed. "What am I to think?" Her gaze searched his. "This was all a joke wasn't it?" Her breath came in quick gasps.

"No, Callie, no," Max began.

Her gaze searched for a way out. The closest was past Bethany. "You made a fool of me, Maxwell Barringer." The words came out louder than she intended.

Silence filled the church.

Rising, she shoved past Bethany and her daughter. They reached for her hand and she jerked it free. She had to flee.

The sound of Max rising to his feet echoed.

"Callie, wait."

But she didn't. Tears blinded her, but she moved with the greatest speed she could muster.

"Callie!" he called again.

But she had found the door. Pushing with all her might, she flung the barrier open and rushed into the town beyond.

"Go after her," Bethany hissed grabbing Max's hand as he stood staring at the open door to the church. "Don't stop until you bring her back."

His mother's urgings forced his feet to move. "Excuse me." Max forced his way past his brother and into the main aisle.

He didn't break eye contact with the door until Seth grabbed his arm.

"Max? What's going on?"

"Tell you later." He pushed Seth's hand away.

Continuing on, Max moved onto the steps of the little church but to his surprise, the street was empty.

"Where could she have gone?" He glanced to the rail; however the horses that belonged to the ranch were still in place.

"Callie," he called and hurried down the steps. "Callie, speak to me."

SHE WASN'T sure where she was going; only that she had to get away. Tears blinded her. One hand holding her skirt, so she wouldn't trip, the other grabbing post to post along the boardwalk as she ran along.

"He knew," she sobbed.

The boardwalk ended and she stumbled as her feet adjusted from the wooden surface the uneven turf of the ground. "Oh, how they must have laughed."

She paused and blindly glanced around. Where

could she go? Who would help her? "I came in from the east. I can go back to Carson City."

She turned around only to run into a solid object.

"Whoa now." A kind voice and someone grabbed her arms. "What's a pretty young thing like you doing running headlong into trouble?"

Callie held fast to the arms that braced her. Blinking to clear the moisture, she focused on the Silver Star displayed proudly on the left side of his vest. "C-can you help me?" she stammered.

"Yes, yes of course, Miss. Come with me."

"ow sit right down here," the man's voice soothed her as he led her into a building and to a chair before his desk.

Callie sank onto the wooden seat and pressed the linen to her face. "I feel like such a fool."

"Well now, if you are a fool, you're the prettiest one I've ever seen."

She hiccuped and watched as he poured a cup of coffee.

"Here now, it's hot."

"Thank you," she murmured and took the thick stoneware mug.

The man was right. The coffee was hot; it nearly burnt her tongue as she took a tiny sip.

"Now, tell me what's going on."

"I don't even know who you are?"

He smiled. "Names Jim McCullough, I'm the sheriff of Rattlesnake Ridge."

"Sheriff." She nodded, as the name rang a bell. "I need to make a complaint."

"All right."

She waited while he opened a drawer and drew out a sheet of paper. Picking his pencil, the sheriff poised it over the paper and asked. "Now, what is the problem?"

"I've been wronged," Callie began.

The man behind the desk stilled.

"I was brought here to marry Seth Nolan," she paused. "Or I thought I was." Callie pressed a hand to her temple. "But it can't be, you see, he's already married."

"Easy now, just start at the beginning and tell me who, what, and where." He pulled out a handkerchief and held it out to her.

Callie took it and blew her nose, then she took a deep breath. Slowly, she began to relate to the officer of the law what had happened.

MOST OF THE congregation stood on the steps or gazed back at Max from below the steps.

"How did this happen?" Seth Nolan demanded.

"It happened because your hands think a lot of you." Max grimaced. "They decided that you needed a wife and set about to find you one."

Seth Nolan looked around the group and noticed three cowboys, heads bent trying to meander away from the church.

"Lou. Teddy. Dill."

At the sound of his voice, the three men increased their strides. They would have made it to their horses, except for the tall man with the star who stepped around a wagon.

"Hey there boys, what's the rush?"

Lou slid to a stop.

The other two men bounced into him unable to halt their forward motion.

"Don't let them get away," Seth called out.

"No, no I don't intend to," McCullough called back. "Gentleman, if you'll hurry back to the church."

Heads down, the three reluctantly moved back toward the gathering.

Seth came down the steps to meet the sheriff. "Jim, it seems my wranglers are in a bit of trouble."

McCullough gave a sharp laugh. "I'd say, they were in a lot of trouble."

A second set of boots hurried down the church steps. "Sheriff, I need you to help me find someone. She's new here and I'm afraid she'll get lost," Max rambled.

"Does she stand about five foot two? Have blonde hair and a broken heart?"

Max nodded. "You know where she is?"

"I do." He looked over to Bethany. "Ma'am." He touched his hat. "I think you ought to come with Max." He glanced over at Reverend Brown. "Reverend, since Winthrop isn't in town today, you too."

"Certainly."

With Nolan herding his wranglers, Bethany, Max and Ida followed along with the sheriff and the minister and his wife.

Samuel Langhorne seized the opportunity to join in the procession. "So tell me, Max, what's going on?"

"Don't answer that," McCullough called back. "You just might perjure yourself."

Max clamped his mouth tight.

Reaching the sheriff's office, McCullough opened the door and ushered the main group inside.

As Langhorne tried to enter, the sheriff put a hand to his chest. "Not right now."

"But the public has a right to know," Langhorne demanded.

"And they will," McCullough winked. "It will be the story of a lifetime." Pushing the newspaper man back, he entered and shut the door. "Everyone sit tight for a moment." The sheriff moved to the front windows and pulled the shades down so that the faces peering in could not see what was going on.

Bethany hurried across the room to where Callie stood her back to all of them and placed her hands on the girl's shoulders. "Callie, honey, are you all right?"

She nodded.

"We were so worried when you left."

McCullough crossed to his desk and picked up a set of keys. "Lou, Teddy, Dill if you'll follow me."

The three forlorn cowboys shuffled their boots against the floor as the sheriff led them through the heavy doors to the cells. The keys clanked against the metal locks which squealed when opened. "Go in, have a seat."

The three walked through and turned to watch McCullough close the doors with a bang.

All eyes were on the sheriff as he moved to his

desk and sat down. "Gentlemen and ladies." He nodded to the women. "We have a problem. This young woman has been brought here under false pretenses. She was under the illusion that she was to be a mail-order bride for one Seth Nolan."

Lou called from the back. "Sheriff. Sheriff, it was my mistake, Sheriff." He stepped forward and hung his arms through the bars. With a quick glance at Callie, he began. "We – me and the boys," he clarified. "We thought if ole Seth got interested in a wife, we'd have a few extra hours off to play hand of cards….or something. We didn't mean no one no harm."

"Hmm," Sheriff McCullough murmured as he sat back in the heavy wooden chair. "So how did you get her here?"

"Well," Lou continued. "We saved our money."

Slowly, the story began to emerge from the borrowing of the books to the pains taken hand written notes.

"But how did Max get involved?" Bethany demanded.

Teddy moved to the bars and grabbing one on each side, he pressed his face up against the cold metal to speak. "That's an easy answer. Max finished school. He had them books by that man, Shakespeare."

Callie went still. "No wonder some of those lines sounded familiar. You-you copied them from his poems."

"Yes ma'am," Teddy admitted. "I'm awful sorry. We didn't mean no harm."

"But harm was done," Callie confronted him. "I have been embarrassed in front of the town."

Teddy hung his head. "I'm sorry, truly I am."

"Who came up with the idea of sending her with Max?" McCullough asked.

"I did." Lou sighed. "She came and the boss done got hitched." He glanced at Ida. "No offense ma'am. We're glad the boss found someone, but it sure made a pickle for us to figure out. By the time she got here, we didn't have a place for her to go. Max…" He glanced at the man in question. "Max here got put in the middle. We – well we knew that Mrs. Barringer and Miss Melinda would be at the ranch. It was sure safer than having her alone in town."

"Safer for you or for Miss McBride?" the sheriff demanded.

All three hung their heads.

"Both," Teddy replied.

"You should be flogged," Mrs. Brown piped up. "Nursed back to health and flogged again. The gall of these men, trifling with a woman's affection. Poetry, from men who can't even recite scripture."

"Now, Mrs. Brown, their hearts were in a good spot," the sheriff mused.

"Poetry couldn't do Callie justice," Max murmured.

His soft voice caused Callie raised her head.

Slowly, Max began to cross toward her. "Callie is the strongest woman I know. She'd let her own happiness take second place." He smiled. "Did you know Seth, she said she'd made a promise to marry you and she wouldn't go back on that promise, even when I sort of asked her."

"Is that right?" Seth grinned as he moved toward his own wife and took her hand.

Callie nodded.

"Then I'm blessed to know two wonderful women. Callie McBride, I release you from your promise to marry me and I hope you can find someone who loves you as deeply as I love my Ida."

Relief flowed through her. Callie gave a shy glance to the sheriff, then shifted her gaze to the man standing next to her. "So what am I supposed to do now?" she whispered.

Max smiled as he walked forward and slipped the handkerchief from her hand. Reaching up, he wiped away the trail of tears that ran down her cheeks. "Did anyone tell you, your eyes are like the lupine blossoms and rival the Nevada sky itself?"

She stared into his eyes and shook her head.

"Or that your laughter rivals the sweetest song of any bird in the meadow."

"No."

"Callie, there's no barrier to keep us apart now. Seth has released you. Lou and his buddies have confessed. I'll ask you in front of these folks and my mother, will you do me the honor of becoming my wife?"

Her smile trembled.

For a moment, everyone held their collective breaths.

Then Callie nodded.

"Yes, yes I'll marry you Maxwell Barringer. I came here to begin a new life and there's no place I'd want to be other than on the Barringer ranch."

A sigh of relief went through the gathered assembly as Max took her into his arms and bestowed a shy kiss upon her lips.

"I love you, Caledonia McBride," Max whispered, as he held her close.

"And I love you," she murmured against his cheek.

Max let her go and slipped his hand over hers. "Reverend Brown, would you be willing to do the honors?"

"Aye son, it will be my pleasure."

"Seth, you'll be my best man?"

"I'd be honored, Max."

"Max," Callie called softly.

"Yes, my dear?"

"You have a cabin to finish."

His grin widened. "So I do."

"Gentleman, there appears to be an urgent need for a house raising up in the foothills of the ranch. I need it done before I walk down the aisle and I'm not waiting more than a week."

"I think that can be arranged." McCullough grinned. "Teddy, Dill, Lou, looks like you found a way to pay off your debt."

"We'll do it, Sheriff, just let us out of here."

McCullough tossed the keys to Seth, who grabbed them and moved to open the cell.

"Oh," McCullough gave a nod to the door. "There's a newspaper man outside that would love to get the scoop on this. I bet if you tell him, you can get a whole lot more people to help with that cabin.

You might even have it finished before the week is out."

"That sounds even better." Max grinned as he swung Callie into another hug.

"I came riding from Richmond and into the arms of love," Callie replied taking hold of his face and kissing him wantonly. "This is the best adventure I could ask for."

EPILOGUE

*C*allie stood outside of the white clapboard church and waited for Barbara to begin Mendelssohn's tune. The white dress she'd brought all the way from Richmond flowed perfectly. Instead of a full veil, Mrs. Handley at the General Store had given her some lace. With the help of Max's mother, she fashioned a short veil that pinned to her hair and hung only down the back. She didn't want to miss a minute of walking down the aisle under Max's gaze.

"Are you nervous?" Melinda asked.

"No. I've never been more sure of anything in my life."

"We're almost ready," Bethany said as she hurried from the front of the church. "But you need something." Reaching down to the bouquet of flowers, picked from the meadow, she pulled two sprigs of lupine. Pulling two hair pins from her own bun, she secured them in place on either side of the veil. "There." Stepping back, Bethany smiled at Callie. "I'm so thrilled to have you as my daughter-in-law. I already love you, like one of my own."

"And I love you," Callie murmured as they embraced.

"Mother," Augustus called.

"Coming." She blew Callie a kissed and then took Augustus' arm. Head held high, they walked into the church.

Melinda stepped forward. "I'll get the back of your dress."

Callie nodded. Together, they walked to the front doors as the notes from the piano filled the air. She looked down the aisle to see Max standing, waiting. Her journey had come to an end. Callie found the love and dreams that would last her a lifetime.

ACKNOWLEDGEMENTS

I would like to thank Melissa Storm and the authors of Pioneer Brides of Rattlesnake Ridge for all the support they have given me. It is an honor to be selected to write one of the first set of novels in a new world. I have gained knowledge and respect for the management of time and the delight in writing. To the cover artist and formatters who bring life to the figments of my imagination, nothing could be any better than what you produced and tweaked. To my beloved editor, you hung with me when I mentioned way too much and helped me shape this wonderful story.

None of this could have been accomplished without their help. I will forever be grateful.

ACKNOWLEDGEMENTS

Nan O'Berry

Read the first chapter of TRAVELING FROM TEXAS, book 5 of the Pioneer Brides of Rattlesnake Ridge…

Tess Cooper stared at her father's scrawled writing. According to the date, he'd written the letter yesterday. She glanced out the door to their small cabin. He'd left early this morning, and the envelope must have fallen out of his pocket. It had not yet been sealed, and not able to resist her curiosity, she'd opened it and read the unsettling words.

She hadn't seen their Uncle Bartholomew in years. Why would Father want to send them away? Nothing made sense. Yet, Father had been acting strangely. Coming home early. Going through Mother's box. What was wrong with him?

Feeling unsteady, she sat down at the table and reread the letter. Why were they in danger? She wished Joe was home so she could ask him. But he was past wild and hadn't come home last night. She stuffed the letter in her pocket, grabbed her shawl, and hurried out the door.

Father was going to have to explain why he would want to send them away. If he was in trouble, they would handle it together. Like they always had.

Halfway into town, she ran into Mattie Quiggins. The old woman gave her a toothless grin and narrowed her eyes. "Lots of folks falling on hard times. Lots of folks leaving Texas."

"Well, I won't. I'll never leave my home. I'm Texas born."

"Yes, you are missy. But most Texans come from somewhere else, and more are leaving to go somewhere else." Mattie grabbed her hand. "I'm old. People talk in front of me because they think I don't matter. But I hear things."

The old woman looked around them and then tugged on Tess's arm. "I saw them yesterday. They were talking. Men that I don't know said they were going to rob the bank."

"When?"

"This morning. Be careful, Missy. I saw the young one ride up to them. He talked, but I couldn't hear him. You know the one. Carl. Don't trust him."

Cold dread worked its way down Tess's spine. Carl? He was her intended. The man she dreamed about and thought she would marry. "That can't be right. Carl wouldn't—"

Old Maggie put a finger to her lips. "They are up to something. I took my money out of the bank, yesterday. Go, quick and tell your father."

Tess pulled away from the old woman.

Maggie wagged her finger. "Better keep an eye on that brother of yours. Saw him going into Kit's saloon. No good can come out of your fast-talking, fast-draw brother, and whiskey."

"I'll speak to Father about him. I'm not his mother." She walked away and wished they still had the horse and carriage. Father kept saying times would get better. So far, they hadn't improved an inch.

Joseph was another story and worry. While Father was gone to war, he'd grown up wild. Mother had tried her best, but he'd become more than she could handle. Then after Mother died, the duty had fallen to her. She'd been no match for her brother.

Father worked hard at the bank, but his wages weren't enough. Little by little, they'd sold off the ranch she knew as home. First the livestock. Then acreage. The house would go next. She would worry, but Father had told her he had it under control.

She was almost to town when she heard her name shouted. Tess turned and saw Joe galloping on a horse toward her.

Joe yanked the horse to a stop and held his arm out to her. "Get on. It's Father."

The fear in her brother's eyes stopped her questions. Tess grabbed hold of Joe's hand and swung up on the back of the prancing horse. She cringed to ask whose animal it was.

Once she had her arms around his waist, he spurred the horse and charged back to town.

"What's wrong?"

"Father's sick."

"What happened?"

"Doc said it's his heart." Joe ran the horse hard all the way back to town and finally stopped him, lathered and blowing, in front of the bank. People were lined up and crowding around the window.

Joe helped her down. "Hurry."

They ran inside the bank where Mr. Harvey, the bank owner, waved them to the back. Tess followed and saw her father on the floor. A jacket under his head.

Doc Baker looked up. He shook his head and stood. "Your father was fighting with someone. He called out, and by the time Mr. Harvey came in, your father was on the floor. The only thing keeping him alive was wanting to talk to you. Better make it quick." The doc took Mr. Harvey, and they left the room.

Her father's face was pale and gray. Tears blurred her vision. "Father—"

"Shh." He put a finger to her lips. "You and Joe, go to Nevada to Uncle Bartholomew. Hurry. Don't wait. Take Joe and leave now."

"Father, you're sick—"

"I'm dying, lass. In Mother's box," He winced and coughed. "Danger. Don't stop for no one."

Tess shook her head and stared at him. "Where—"

"Uncle, Rattlesnake Ridge, Nevada. Joe take her." Father closed his eyes, coughed again, and stopped breathing.

Tess threw herself onto him. "No."

Joe grabbed her. "We better go." He pulled her up. Holding her close, he helped her out of the bank. "We need to get home and leave."

She looked back. "But Father—"

"We have to go." Joe put her on the horse and climbed up behind her. "I barely remember Uncle Bartholomew."

She leaned against him. "Father had said he was a prominent citizen in the town. I guess he can help us get started again." Tears wetted her cheeks. "Why do you think Father wanted us—"

"Don't ask. We'll just do what he said." Joe spoke as a man and not the wild boy she knew. Quiet and in their own thoughts, they rode home.

Joe kept a hand on his pistol and looked around. "We better hurry."

Tess followed him into the house. Nevada. Just where was that anyway? West was all she knew.

Joe pulled the box down and opened it. He gasped and held up a bag. "Gold coins and hundred-dollar bills. Must be five thousand dollars in here."

"How did Father get that kind of money?" She tried to answer the question and still think of her father as the honorable man she'd always known.

Joe stared at it. "Think he stole it?"

"Father isn't a thief."

"No. But he didn't have this kind of money either, and Mr. Harvey said someone had come in and had cross words with him right before his heart gave out."

She looked through the box, but everything else was as it should be. Mother's ring. Her brooch. Locks of hair from her and Joe.

Joe stood and grabbed the rifle and cartridges. "Pack a few things. We have to go."

"Who would want to hurt us?"

He stopped at the door. "I saw some men in the saloon. Heard words and mention of Father's name. We don't want to be around when they come looking for this money."

Fear shadowed her as she went into her room and pulled the satchel from under her bed. What had Father done? Tess glanced around her room. So many memories lingered in the small cabin they called home. After packing, she sat on her bed and listened. It was a game she played late at night. She could imagine her mother calling out, Father answering, and Joe laughing. Life in the Cooper home was often loud and full of laughter. Used to be, anyway.

Tess frowned. But no more. Mother was gone. Now Father.

"Tess, we need to go."

She went out and saw Joe standing by the door. Rifle in one hand, knapsack in the other. He'd changed. No longer the wild boy, he looked the part of a man with responsibility. Something very new to her brother.

Joe gave her a grim smile. "I'll saddle Father's horse for you. He must have walked into town today. I'll turn the cow loose."

"Do you think we have to go?"

He nodded and watched outside. "Father said it for a reason. Said we were in danger. Watch for me. When I bring the horse out, you come outside." He handed her the rifle. "I don't know what danger we're looking for, but we better be ready."

Tess took the gun and stayed in the doorway. Growing up in Texas had made her wary and ready. There'd been a time that they had to watch for Indians. Now, it was the lawless men who'd been ruined by the war and hard times.

She wondered about Father. Is that what had happened to him? They'd struggled ever since the war. If it wasn't the Yankees, it was the carpetbaggers. Add high taxes and a ruined economy, and so many were struggling to survive.

"Oh, Father. What did you do?"

Joe walked up with Brandywine behind him. "He's ready for you." He helped her mount and then jumped on his horse. "I figure we ride to Dallas. There's bound to be trains we can take. We'll sell the horses."

She rubbed Brandywine's neck. The horse was a beauty with a dark red coat and black mane and tail. He was also Father's source of pride. "Do we have to get rid of him, too?"

"We can buy new ones in Nevada."

"I'd like to say goodbye to Carl." Just the last month, she'd begun to think there might be more than friendship between them. He worked at the bank with her father and would soon know of her father's death. In fact, she found it strange that he hadn't been at the bank this morning. Then again, there was Maggie's odd warning.

Joe shook his head. "No. Not until we know what we're up against. Father wouldn't have said we had to leave now if he hadn't meant it. I'm responsible to look after you."

"But I owe Carl a goodbye." She was beginning to come out of the shock of the events and get angry.

"Father told me to take care of you, and that's what I'm going to do. Once I deliver you to Uncle

Bartholomew, then you can do what you want." He glanced around.

She noticed how uneasy her brother had become. "You don't think someone is out to kill us?"

Joe stared at her. "Carl and Father had cross words this morning. I think Carl caused his heart attack, and then he ran out of the bank. I'm not taking a chance. Father made me responsible for you."

"Carl? But we were talking marriage."

Joe patted his pocket. "We might not have broken the law, but I'm not so sure about Father, and really not sure about Carl."

"Father wouldn't do anything wrong. He wouldn't."

Joe just shrugged. "That money came from somewhere, and Carl argued with Father enough to make his heart give out. We do what Father wanted."

Seeing her brother wasn't going to budge, she nodded. "Let's go. Your horse is tired though. We better just walk."

He grinned. "You always watch out for the animals, don't you? Yeah, I already thought of it. I'll buy another one soon as we come to a place."

"With what? We don't have but ten dollars between us."

Joe glanced at her with a wry grin. "I'd say we about five thousand dollars."

"We are not bank robbers."

"No, but we aren't going to sit around here and get killed over this money either."

Tess knew to argue further was pointless. Later, they'd come to an agreement about what to do with Father's money.

Joe took her north away from the main road and led her through fields green from spring rains. Tears threatened as she thought of her father dying. Now to lose their home, too. And be threatened by some unknown danger.

She sighed. "I hope Uncle Bartholomew remembers us. Before Mother died, she'd received a letter from him. He said he was doing well in the town of Rattlesnake Ridge. What a name for a town."

Joe swung his horse around to ride beside her. "Maybe he's the town mayor. Anyway, it's a good thing that he'll be able to help us." He stopped under a tree. "Let's rest the horses a bit."

Tess studied her brother. Before this morning, he'd been a happy-go-lucky boy who didn't have a care in the world. Now, she could see the worry in his blue eyes. They were icy-blue like Father's. Joe was a handsome, tall, muscular man, but his face was still boyish. Not hardened like men who'd faced hard lives.

She faced him. "Joe, I think we should pray."

He stared at her as anger and sorrow flitted across his face. "Didn't help Mother much."

Tess took great comfort in her faith and wasn't going to let her brother's doubts stop her. "From what we know, I think we could use some Divine guidance and protection."

He looked away. "Go ahead. I won't stop you. We're resting the horses anyway."

"Joe, it's important."

"Go ahead."

She bowed her head. "Father in heaven, watch over us. Protect us and guide us to Rattlesnake Ridge. Prepare Uncle Bartholomew's heart to receive us and help us. Take care of Father for us. Amen."

Tess thought she heard a whispered "amen" from Joe, but she didn't want to press him. She'd struggled since Mother's death and the hard times, too. But Tess always knew the Lord was with her and could feel His Presence in the quiet times. She said a silent prayer for Joe that he'd remember the faith

Mother had instilled in them since they were little. She had a feeling they were going to need it.

"Let's go." Joe moved out from under the trees and looked to make sure she was following.

Tess rode up beside him. "I think we should send a letter to Uncle Bartholomew, so he knows that we're coming. I don't want to send him Father's letter. I want us to have a fresh start in the town."

"All right. You write it." He started to say more but instead shook his head, and then looked back over the trail they'd taken.

His actions unsettled her. Did he really believe someone would be following them? "How long before we reach Dallas?"

Joe shrugged and then stopped. "I got a feeling that's not where we should go. We have the money. I think we'd be better off to go to Arkansas. Catch a train north to Kansas and then go west." He grinned. "First thing we need to do is figure out where Rattlesnake Ridge is."

Tess sighed. "A long way away is all I know."

"Carl, or anyone following won't expect us to go east."

"I wish I could have talked to Carl. We were kind of close. In time, I even thought he might ask me to marry him."

Joe stared at her. "I never liked him."

"Why?"

He shook his head. "I'm not sure. He didn't seem truthful. Like he was always hiding something. Forget about him."

Tess considered her brother's words. There had been something about Carl that had kept her from trusting him. But then again, in light of what had happened today, it might be hard for her to trust anyone again. "I did like him."

Joe nailed her with a serious look. "Best if you put him out of your mind. Doubtful you'll ever see him again anyway."

Angry at being pushed around, Tess grabbed his reins. "You might be responsible for my safety, but you are not my boss. I don't like you telling me what to do."

He shook his head. "You are the feisty one." He touched the tip of her nose. "Probably one of the reasons Carl hadn't asked for your hand yet." He turned serious again. "After today, I'm glad he didn't."

"I mean it, Joe. We're equal in this. I want to be a part of our plans."

Joe yanked his reins from her hand and took several steps away before he stopped and turned to face her. "All right, we're partners. Equal partners. Not like I could imagine telling you what to do anyway. God help the man who sets his sights on you."

She gasped. "How dare you talk to me like that."

He grinned. "It's truthful. You're one independent woman. A pretty one though." He pulled her horse along. "Come on. We need to work together. Let's get to a train station that can get us north."

He was right. If men were after them, it was prudent to be on the move. She kicked the horse and surged past Joe. "Catch me if you can." She galloped along the trail, dodging tree limbs, and jumping fallen logs and ditches. She loved to ride and ride fast.

Today she needed to. She needed to leave behind the heartache. To ride fast away from losing her father, her home, even Carl.

Finally, she slowed and waited for Joe. He had stayed back and was in no hurry. He caught up to her and ushered her behind a stand of trees. He put his fingers to his lips and took the rifle from the scabbard.

Tess tried to see between the branches. "Did you spot a deer?" Her stomach rumbled, and she thought about how they did need to eat.

Joe shook his head.

She started to move beyond the trees to see better when Joe grabbed her reins.

"Stay. Someone's following us."

A chill swept through her. "Who?"

He shook his head and gestured for her to be quiet. Joe dismounted and put his hands over the muzzles of both horses.

The April sun beat through the trees pouring heat down on them. Tess closed her eyes and prayed. Surely, they wouldn't be caught this soon. And how could anyone know the direction they'd have taken?

She heard the steady clop of a trotting horse and held her breath. Through the leaves, she caught sight of a gray horse with black socks. She knew that horse. And as she watched, she saw Carl ride past them.

Joe looked at her and mouthed for her to stay put. Rifle in hand, he walked out of the trees and onto the trail. "Carl."

Carl whirled his horse around. "Joe, I was looking for Tess. Her father — "

"We know."

"I had to find out if Tess was all right." Carl looked around. "Is she with you?"

Tess kept quiet. Something about the way Carl was looking around bothered her. Carl looked concerned, but even from where she was standing, she doubted he was worried about her. He was after the money.

"Where is she? I stopped by your house."

Joe stood his ground, keeping the rifle ready. "She's visiting a relative. Father's death hit her hard."

"You drop her off in Fort Worth?"

"What do you want Carl?"

"Your father said she might have something of mine, and I care about your sister. I want to make sure she's all right."

Joe nodded. "I'll tell her. She'll contact you when she's through mourning our father's death."

Carl frowned, finally shrugged, and turned his horse. "Tell her I'll be in touch." He rode away, never looking back.

Joe waited out in the open with rifle in hand.

After Carl had ridden out of view, Tess led the horses to Joe. "Why didn't you want me to talk to him?"

"Just a feeling. Things I've heard."

Tess's knees were weak. "He had Father's pipe

in his pocket. Did you see that? He must have been at our house looking for the money."

Joe nodded with sadness in his eyes. He ushered her and the horses back behind the trees. "Just the other day at Kit's, Carl came into the saloon with another man. One I hadn't seen before. He was bragging about the bank. Said he knew things. Then he saw me and hushed up."

She darted a look down the trail. Carl was coming back, but this time he had a gun drawn.

Joe swung her up on her horse and then mounted his. "Go, don't look back. Meet me at the lazy oak. If I don't come, you go on to Uncle Bartholomew's." He took the satchel from his saddle and handed it to her. "Take it and go. I'll meet up with you." He slapped her horse.

Tess looked back and saw Joe riding away from her. She darted through the brush on the faint trail that she and Joe knew so well. Growing up they'd played on horseback. Chasing one another. Hiding and then trailing each other for practice.

Periodically, she stopped and listened, but no one was following her. Finally, she saw the lazy oak. The tree was bent and growing parallel to the ground. As kids, she and Joe had made up stories as to what had happened to the tree.

Her favorite story had been of a dragon who wanted to rest and leaned on the tree and his great weight bent it until he fashioned it a chair and sat on, forcing it to go perpendicular to the ground before finally reaching for the skies.

Two shots rumbled in the distance. Tess bowed her head and prayed, hoping her brother was safe. Her heart raced as time slid by, her fear mounting. The sun slipped behind the ridge casting shadows along the land and on her hopes.

The moon was rising when she heard hoofbeats in the distance. They came closer.

Wishing she had a gun, Tess peered through the branches.

Joe rode to the tree and jumped down. His lip and cheek were bloody. But it was the sad look in his eyes that scared her.

"You didn't hurt Carl?"

"Not much. Just enough to learn what I needed to know." He took his canteen and sipped a long drink. "He said he was in on it with Father to take that money. That we owe him half of it."

"I don't believe it." Tess's heart reeled from the love for her father mixed with anger and betrayal.

"It's what Carl said. What he said with a gun in

his face. We better go. I don't trust Carl not to follow us."

Tess took a hanky and dabbed at his bloodied lip. "Carl wouldn't hurt me."

Joe stared at her. "I don't want you to ever think about him again. He's not to be trusted."

The harsh way Joe spoke made his words count in her mind. She did trust Joe. "What are we going to do?"

He stared at her. "We're going to Rattlesnake Ridge and find Uncle Bartholomew. Then we'll be safe."

Tess shuddered at the way her brother spoke. She leaned against the old tree and prepared to live a new life. Watching the bright moon, she prayed that Uncle Bartholomew could help them. She prayed Joe would stay out of trouble in the new town. Finally, she prayed that the Lord would give them a fresh start.

Want to keep reading? Head to sweetpromisepress.com/PioneerBrides to grab your copy now!

What's our Sweet Promise? It's to deliver the heart-warming, entertaining, clean, and wholesome reads you love with every single book.

From contemporary to historical romances to suspense and even cozy mysteries, all of our books are guaranteed to put a song in your heart and a smile on your face. That's our promise to you, and we can't wait to deliver upon it...

We release one new book per week, which means the flow of sweet, relatable reads coming your way never ends. Make sure to save some space on your eReader!

Check out our books in Kindle Unlimited at
sweetpromisepress.com/Unlimited

Download our free app to keep up with the latest releases and unlock cool bonus content at sweetpromisepress.com/App

Join our reader discussion group, meet our authors, and make new friends at sweetpromisepress.com/Group

Sign up for our weekly newsletter at sweetpromisepress.com/Subscribe

And don't forget to like us on Facebook at sweetpromisepress.com/FB

THE *Pioneer Brides* OF RATTLE SNAKE RIDGE

Sweet Promise

Their fortunes lie out west...and so do their hearts.

ARRIVING FROM ARKANSAS BY ELISA KEYSTON

Josephine Lane arrived in Rattlesnake Ridge under false pretenses. As far as the townspeople know, she's simply the new cook for the local boarding house. Nobody has to know the secret her late uncle shared with her before his death or how that same secret could make her the wealthiest person in the state of Nevada.

Jim Griffin works hard as a foreman at the local lumber mill. He also works hard to keep his real identity as an undercover lawman hidden as he closes in on his brother's murderer. When the killer gets close, the last thing Jim needs is a distraction–

especially the pretty blonde cook at the boarding house.

Jim and Josie's separate secrets just might bring them closer than either could have predicted. But will they be able to resist falling in love when so much is already at stake for the both of them?

If you like historical romance with a touch of intrigue, then you'll love Arriving from Arkansas. Get your copy and start reading today!

Get your copy at
sweetpromisepress.com/PioneerBrides

COMING FROM CALIFORNIA BY CATHERINE BILSON

When Daisy Jackson applied for the role of Rattlesnake Ridge's new schoolmistress, she may have omitted a few important details, like her young age and lack of teaching experience. And it certainly doesn't help that the town council holds her mixed-ethnicity against her, too.

Luke Rockford fell head over heels the very moment he laid eyes on Daisy, but he wasn't the only one. His rival, Deputy Grant Watson also set his sights on the pretty teacher. The arrogant lawman is accustomed to getting what he wants, even if he has to bend the rules to claim it, from the job promised to Luke to any woman in town.

With so much to do before the school year begins, Daisy hardly knows which way to turn. Can she put down roots and fall in love before the town council runs her out of Rattlesnake Ridge?

If you like strong female characters, cheeky cowboys, and dastardly deputies then you're sure to enjoy reading Coming from California. Get your copy to learn which man wins Daisy's heart!

Get your copy at
sweetpromisepress.com/PioneerBrides

MOVING FROM MARYLAND BY CHRISTINE STERLING

Gracie Pickett followed her dreams of being a physician all the way to Rattlesnake Ridge. Learning the trade was the easy part, however. Convincing the small pioneer town that she's up to the job is the tough part, especially when a rude, arrogant, oh-so-handsome widower and his three adorable boys seem to make it their mission to make her new life far more difficult than she ever anticipated.

Barrett Wright is busy managing his under-staffed ranch while also hoping to find a wife to tend to his rambunctious sons. When the town council tasks him with finding a new doctor, he finds the perfect man for the job—until he learns the new doctor is a woman! Barrett is determined to see Gracie replaced with someone more suitable, if only he can tear his eyes away from her long enough to get the job done.

Gracie has no intention of giving up her new practice. When an accident puts her medical skills to the test, will she be able to prove to her biggest rival that she's the right person for the job... and his heart?

If you like enemies-to-lovers plots in historical settings, then you're sure to love Moving from Maryland. Grab your copy and start reading today!

Get your copy at
sweetpromisepress.com/PioneerBrides

RIDING FROM RICHMOND by NAN O'BERRY

Caledonia McBride thought war destroyed her chance at happiness. But then an ad for marriageable women offers hope for a second chance, and soon letters from a lonely rancher fill her heart. Ready for a second chance, Caledonia pulls up her Virginia roots and travels west toward the promise of a new beginning.

Maxwell Barringer is a good friend. When three well-meaning ranch hands accidentally bring a young woman to town to be the bride of a man who's already married, he steps in to help his friends save face until they can raise the money to send her back to Virginia. The only problem is, the more he gets to know Miss Caledonia McBride, the harder it is for him to imagine her leaving.

As Caledonia settles into her new life at Rattlesnake Ridge, it's only a matter of time before the truth comes out. Can Max untangle the web before he falls for the blue-eyed beauty?

If you enjoy the romantic adventures of mail-order-brides, then you'll love Riding from Richmond. Get your copy and start reading now!

Get your copy at
sweetpromisepress.com/PioneerBrides

~

Traveling from Texas by Patricia PacJac Carroll

Tess Cooper fled Texas after her father's dying words warned that remaining would spell danger. Setting their sights on Rattlesnake Ridge, she and her brother look forward to making a fresh start, but that same family secret could ruin their new lives before they even arrive.

Jacob Winthrop has his hands full. In addition to raising his eight-year-old daughter and running a business, he's also the mayor of Rattlesnake Ridge. Finding someone to mother his child would help, but he has no interest in making a commitment— until he meets Tess.

But secrets stand in the way, making fresh starts impossible for Tess, and she doesn't want her troubles to hurt Jacob's reputation.

If you like reading a tender romance thwarted by secrets and set in a small town with small-town troubles then you'll love Traveling from Texas. Grab it and start reading now!

Get your copy at sweetpromisepress.com/PioneerBrides

Drifting from Deadwood by Ramona Flightner

Eleanor Ferguson has little faith in the promises of men after her husband's death leaves her with a floundering ranch and two growing boys. Her top priority is to create a legacy for her sons, but a greedy neighbor has other plans. When a drifter answers her help wanted ad, she doesn't expect to feel attraction for the handsome stranger.

Lance Gallagher drifts from ranch to ranch until life leads him to Rattlesnake Ridge, Nevada. He's willing to work for low wages on the Ferguson ranch until the mines deliver on their promise of a payout. The more time Lance spends with Eleanor and her sons, however, the more attracted he finds himself to the lovely widow. Unwilling to risk his heart, he makes plans to leave.

Then tragedy strikes, forcing Eleanor and Lance to rely on each other. Can they overcome their fears and learn to trust in love again?

If you enjoy friends-to-lovers historical romances, then you'll love Drifting from Deadwood. Grab your copy and start reading today!

Get your copy at
sweetpromisepress.com/PioneerBrides

Indigo Springs Series

Contemporary Western Romance

Love comes happily ever after, if you follow your hearts dreams. In Indigo Springs, Texas, that's what awaits the three Malone brothers. Come meet Logan Malone and his brothers, Jason and Troy as they navigate true love's often bumpy course.

Three Rivers Station

Historical Western Romance

The Express took men and rode them hard across the West. That adventuring spirit belonged to the men, full of life, ready for whatever met them on the trail, everything, except for love.

First Street Church

Sweet and Wholesome

Small town love stories with the community church at their center of their lives and make for the perfect feel-good reads!

ABOUT THE AUTHOR

Home is where the heart lies. Or so Nan O'Berry believes. She grew up on a quiet street in Virginia Beach, Virginia, however her love of horses led her family to purchase a small farm in the Western Tidewater area. She grew up listening to family tales, so it was not surprising that she loves a great story.

Armed with a Bachelor's degree in Interdisciplinary Studies from Old Dominion University, she loves sharing heroic stories of cowboys, Texas Rangers, lumberjacks, and just plain, small town folks.

Made in the USA
Middletown, DE
07 May 2021

38555143R00170